The Women Friends: Selina

Emma Rose Millar
&
Miriam Drori

Finalist: Chanticleer Goethe Award for
Late Historical Fiction

CROOKED
CAT

First Blue Line Edition
Crooked Cat Publishing Ltd. 2016

Discover us online:
www.crookedcatbooks.com

Join us on facebook:
www.facebook.com/crookedcatbooks

*Tweet a photo of yourself holding
this book to @crookedcatbooks
and something nice will happen.*

About the Authors

Emma Rose Millar was born in Birmingham – a child of the seventies. She is a single mum and lives with her young son who keeps her very busy and very happy. Emma left school at 16 and later studied for an Open University degree in Humanities with English Literature. She has had a variety of jobs including chocolatier, laboratory technician and editorial assistant for a magazine, but now works part-time as an interpreter.

Emma writes historical fiction and children's picture books, winning the Legend category of the Chaucer Awards with *Five Guns Blazing* in 2014. She is currently working on her third novel, *Jezebel*, a dark tale of obsession and opium addiction set in the roaring twenties.

Emma is an avid fan of live music and live comedy and enjoys skating, swimming and yoga.

For more information, please visit:
https://emmarosemillar.com/
or follow Emma's author page on Amazon:
http://author.to/EmmaRoseMillar

Miriam Drori was born and raised in London, but has lived most of her life in Jerusalem, where she married and gave birth to three now grown-up children. Following careers in computer programming and technical writing, Miriam turned her attention to creative writing. Her first published novel, *Neither Here Nor There*, is a romance set in Jerusalem, a story of two people drawn to each other despite their very different backgrounds.

Miriam began writing in order to raise awareness of social anxiety and never fails to mention this common but little-known disorder when the opportunity arises.

You can find out more about Miriam and connect with her on her website/blog:
https://miriamdrori.com/
or follow her author page on Amazon:
http://Author.to/MiriamDroriAtAmazon

Emma's and Miriam's other titles by Crooked Cat:

Five Guns Blazing by Emma Rose Millar
Neither Here Nor There by Miriam Drori

Acknowledgements

We would like to thank Crooked Cat Publishing for agreeing to publish *The Women Friends: Selina,* and all of their authors for being so supportive. Thank you to Laurence Patterson at Soqoqo Design for a wonderful cover, and to Stephanie Patterson and our editor Jeff Gardiner for all their hard work on the manuscript.

Last, but by no means least, we would like to give a huge thank you to all our lovely friends and family who have given us so much support and encouragement with the whole project.

The Women Friends: Selina

In 1917, Gustav Klimt painted his sensuous masterpiece *The Women Friends*. Nothing is known about the two women in the painting, but it is thought they were a real couple. The tragic fate of the painting itself and ominous developments in Vienna in the early twentieth-century inspired us to write a series of stories, based on Klimt's women and some of his most renowned work.

Emma Rose Millar & Miriam Drori

Chapter One

I arrived in Vienna in 1916 on a steam locomotion that wound its way through the Austrian countryside with its lush hills and its pastel villages. I was just a young woman then, with only my dreams and an invitation to model for the notorious fashion salon, Schwestern Flöge. I remember sitting there in the airless carriage with the windows up and the grey veil of smoke swirling past me as the train gathered speed, racing away from Tyrol; away from all I had known. To my left was a narrow corridor where people hurried back and forth in search of seats.

"Entschuldigen Sie bitte," they mumbled as they navigated past one another.

There was a rectangular mirror opposite and a rolled up blind at the window, racks for luggage, and a glass lamp whose shade had yellowed with heat. I could hear a muffled conversation somewhere: "The Russians will be pushed back from Poland by the end of the month, and I'd bet my last Krone Romania will be next. The war will be over by Christmas; you wait."

I was sick of it. I rested my head against the juddering window frame and watched as the forests grew darker and my reflection became vivid in the glass, alarmed by the dread I saw in the face that stared back at me. I was too young for all this; my family were back in the village. *Too late to go back now.* I was frightened, I was alone and I didn't have the fare to go home. I'd earn it soon enough, I supposed, in Vienna, where the streets were paved with gold and a girl's face was her fortune.

"Ticket please, Fräulein." The voice shook my thoughts from me and I fumbled fretfully inside my purse until at last

I pulled out a little square of pink card. I should never have left Tyrol.

It was almost midnight when the train eventually came screaming into Vienna Westbahnhof with its steam billowing and brakes hissing between the two white towers that flanked the main hall. I looked up as I alighted and heaved my case onto the almost empty platform, up towards the arched window right at the top of one of the towers, wishing he was here with me. Leon. He could have come with me, on this big adventure to the city, but instead I'd probably never see him again.

The last time I saw him it was snowing and we walked hand in hand along the cobbles, between the sherbet-coloured buildings, icicles hanging from their balconies like swords. The Alps soared up abruptly at the end of the street. The weavers and the chocolate factory were all shut up. My mouth was shut up. We'd been in his room again, it was the same every time. I thought I could do it; he kissed me, slowly, gently and ran his tongue around my earlobe and down the line of my throat, leaving a hot trail that went cold, goose pimples springing up in its wake.

"Are you alright, Selina?"

I nodded and looked into his eyes which were brown like mine, but not like mine. They were warm – they made him look sad, almost, and lost. He slid his thigh between my legs and his hands were pushing at my skirt. He hooked his thumbs around the sides of my knickers; I could feel his breath against my cheek. At once, it all seemed horrible and ugly again. In panic, I grabbed him around his wrist.

"I can't, Leon," I told him. "I can't do it, I'm sorry."

"Jesus!" He flung himself from me.

"I can't." I felt my eyes grow hot and prickly, and then there was the crushing sense of embarrassment and shame.

"Selina, you can't keep doing this; other men won't be as patient as me." He put his arm around my shoulder and I felt myself folding inwards and hiding my face in his chest, trying desperately to block out the memory of what they'd done. "Has somebody hurt you?"

I shook my head, wondering how I'd let myself get to this point again. I loved Leon. I wanted him. Every time I thought it might be alright, and yet somehow the fear that swept over me was all too much, and before I knew it I'd be struggling and fighting him like an alley cat. *It was your brothers,* I wanted to scream, but I daren't. I daren't tell him for fear of losing him. How stupid could I have been? I'd lost him already.

"You do know I'm marrying Giselle?"

I couldn't speak.

"I'm going to marry her." He held my hand and I wound my fingers tightly around his. "This can't go on. Jesus Christ, Selina." He stood up and shook his trousers, adjusting himself uncouthly. "You're just like a little girl."

I felt my cheeks grow hot and turned my face from him.

We walked silently along the cobbles and turned down the dirt-track that led to my parents' door. When I turned to look at him I found myself standing all alone under the lamplight and Leon was gone. I called after him, but my voice was carried away and rang hauntingly around the unforgiving mountains. He never came back for me.

Now, here I was alone again, at the station, standing on the platform with my battered suitcase clutched in one hand and a crumpled piece of paper with *Waldstrasse 101,* my new address, scribbled on it, held tightly in the other.

Back in Tyrol people said I was beautiful; Leon said I was beautiful, but obviously not beautiful enough, not in the end. Not for him anyway.

"A man has needs, Selina." Those were his parting words. *A man has needs.* What the hell was that supposed to mean?

I made my way slowly up the stone steps into the street, which was lit by gas lamps and still bustling with people, smart men and women spilling out of coffee houses, shadowy figures pedalling past the theatre. I'd never seen so many people – not so late at night, but even at this hour the city was bathed in a kind of twilight. There was not the darkness of the countryside where the slightest sound was amplified and a person couldn't even dream of venturing out after sundown without a lamp. I stuck my hand out for a passing cab and thrust my papers in through the open window. The driver nodded at me impassively; I may just as well have been invisible. I sat on the back seat while he smoked and turned the steering wheel with his free hand.

"This is it," he eventually said and he pulled up outside a towering building with dark windows and a crumbling roof. When I thought of those candy-coloured buildings in Tyrol with their sprawling balconies and hanging baskets at their doors I could have cried. This place was falling to pieces. I sighed. I paid the driver and dragged my belongings out onto the pavement.

Inside, the atmosphere was loud and gay. I could hear chatter and raucous laughter coming from somewhere. It echoed as I walked along the tiled lobby. There was a polished counter to the right, behind which lay a bureau. The space was so small yet into it were crammed all sorts of colourful characters: women in furs who looked to be actresses or prostitutes; young boys – it was all very odd – and all of them fawning over a man who, judging by his uniform, seemed to be some kind of concierge for the building. He was a strange-looking person with hair that appeared to have been groomed with Brilliantine and combed into a peak at the front. I was sure he was wearing rouge, and kohl around his eyes. His expression was sad. I looked at his name badge: *Jonas Lehner.* He'd been stuffed into little more than a cubby hole, where tenants' mail was kept securely and keys were checked in and out according to the various comings and goings.

"Name?" he asked, only glancing at me for the briefest of moments.

My throat was hoarse from the journey. "Selina Brunner."

"Room fourteen." He handed me a key with a rectangular fob. "On the fifth floor."

I'd thought he might help me, but he was far too engrossed with his entourage. My luggage bumped against each step as I ascended the spiral staircase, clinging to the sweeping banister, until wearily I reached my floor and opened the door to number fourteen. It was a sparse little room with a stone basin for washing, a small sofa, which was worn and saggy, a single bed, and a kind of kitchen area off with two cupboards, a sink with a drainer and a veneer counter. I dumped my suitcase down beside the bed. The place was dirty. Other people may not have noticed it, I supposed, but I was very meticulous that way. I found myself a cloth from the kitchen cupboard and gave the skirting boards a wipe over. But there was grime in the crevices around the window frame and where the draining board met the work surface. I wrapped a knife in the cloth and chipped away at it. The window, too, was smutty, as was the mirror which hung on the back of the door. There was a layer of grease and what looked like talcum powder over everything. The dirt seemed to cling everywhere. I couldn't get it off; I'd have to buy vinegar to clean the glass, which would be no inconvenience, since I liked to soak my meat in it anyway. It got rid of all the germs... And some new cloths as well, as I'd worn that one threadbare.

The thought of the vinegar and the cloths seemed to calm me. I lay down on my bed and let myself sink into the mattress, which was musty and smelled of dust. It was not at all like Leon's bed, which was soft and warm and smelled faintly of aftershave and the sweat of a working man. *At least, he'll be enjoying some convivial society!* The tormenting image hung there, and I felt my thoughts grow bitter. Men could be so infuriatingly predictable! He'd forgotten all about me already, I was sure, back in Tyrol, playing house with that saggy, sallow-faced old bore. I thought of his face with his crooked smile and his hazel-coloured hair and I shut my eyes and cried into my pillow. What on earth had I done?

By the time I stirred the next morning, the corridor was

9

already alive with fleeting conversations and the tread of high heeled shoes along the boards. I could hear windows being opened in the room above and the sound of running water somewhere. There was a faint tapping at my door that grew louder, showing no sign of abating. I flung back my covers and padded towards the door, opening it just a crack.

"Selina Brunner?" inquired a young woman from the passageway. She was very blonde, and her hair was cut in the new bobbed style which sat just at her jaw and was tucked behind her ear to reveal some sparkly earrings. "From Tyrol?" She put me in mind of a choir boy, she was so sweet-looking.

I nodded and opened the door wider to allow her in. There was another girl with her whose hair was black as a raven and also bobbed, although it had a much more severe look to it.

"Livia," said the blonde one by way of introduction. She was ugly when she smiled. Her smile was insincere; it was small and pinched and her eyes quite dispassionate as she formed it upon her lips. "And this is my friend Neomi. We also work for Fräulein Flöge and have a room here, upstairs, although we have to share ours, don't we, Neomi?" She turned to her friend with that same dishonest smile. Then she ran her finger along the foot of my bed and rubbed the dust away with her thumb. "You're very brown, aren't you? Like a nut. I suppose that must come from living all those years in the countryside. We're so cooped up here in the city, aren't we, Neomi? We never see the outdoors until the moon comes up and the gas lamps are lit!" Her eyes flitted up towards my hair which was tied up in rags. Her friend didn't utter a word although I thought I saw the two of them exchange some kind of look.

"Vienna's very different from Tyrol," I conceded. "I suppose I'll soon get used to it."

"Indeed," said Livia. "Do you have any coffee at all? Or chocolate?"

"Just a little coffee," I told her, "in my suitcase."

There was a silence, which lingered on until

awkwardness forced me to ask them whether they might care for a cup. They both smiled and sat down on my bed. Livia took a packet of cigarettes from her purse and offered one to Neomi. They shared a light from a card of matches. Livia smiled again and said, "You don't, do you, Selina? Smoke, I mean? You country-girls never do."

"No."

"Do you want to try some?" asked Neomi. "All the French models are doing it these days."

I took the cigarette from her with apprehension as she made encouraging nods, but when I drew from it I coughed so hard I went all light-headed and thought I might be sick. They exchanged *that look* again and laughed until the sound of them made me quite uncomfortable.

Once they'd finished their coffee, Livia said we should be on our way to the studio. I quickly emptied the ashtray and washed it out in the sink. I did so hate the smell of a stale ashtray about the place. They took me along what seemed like a secret passage in the boarding house to an elevator with a sliding grille at its entrance. Inside, the walls were cladded with a walnut veneer and there was a slim pot in the corner holding a bouquet of synthetic lilies. We alighted at what looked like some kind of tradesman's door which led out onto a backstreet where the dustbins were kept. Neomi and Livia walked arm in arm round to the front of the building with me trailing at their heels. The Strasse was all bustle, a hum of movement; cyclists navigating their way in and out of the traffic, and pedestrians weaving their way along the cobbles. Livia and Neomi were laughing again and had turned back in the direction from which we'd come. There was a large man hurrying towards us, wearing a white shirt with beads of sweat glistening on his brow, and thinning hair which looked as if he might have grown it in order to cover a bald patch.

"Fräuleins!" he shouted after them. "The rent, please. You're very overdue."

Their laughter didn't stop even for a moment and Livia hailed a passing taxi cab – a Renault which pulled up at the kerb.

"Beg your pardon, Herr Auer," she shouted, opening the cab door. His pace quickened as she ducked inside the car and tucked her skirt in under her thighs.

"Yes, sorry, Herr Auer," Neomi called along the street to him, "but we're running a little late this morning and can't possibly stop. We still haven't received our wages for the job we did last week but our patron assures us we shall be paid in full tomorrow, when we shall of course settle our bill."

She, too, dipped inside the cab and pulled me in after her, slamming the door shut. "Mariahilfer Strasse," she instructed the driver, "and keep your foot off the break." The taxi sped off and I saw Herr Auer fading into the distance through the back window. He tore up a piece of paper and trampled it under his shoe.

We could have walked to the studio; Mariahilfer Strasse was only two blocks away.

"These cobbles pay havoc with a girl's shoes!" said Livia. "And Neomi simply can't go anywhere in this humidity with her hair! It's coarse as a brush once the damp gets into it, isn't it, dear? We could do with a good storm, to clear this rotten air a bit." She smiled at me. "The new girl always pays the cab fare on her first day." Her look was quite expectant and she tapped her foot as I fumbled inside my purse. I pulled out a five Krone note and she appeared satisfied. "Keep the change," she told the driver.

It wasn't until I'd been in Vienna for a few days, living side by side with the other girls, that I could see how inelegant and artless I really was. We stood day after day, in turns under the glare of the spot lamp or the shade of the umbrella looking either into or away from the clicking shutter. The photographer periodically stuck his head out from behind the folding bellows and demanded, "More zing, ladies," or "Less racy! It's frocks you're selling, not what's inside them!"

The studio was small and glaringly white. There were

plinths all covered with white silk, upon which women dressed in the salon's clothes were draped. It was a strange style of couture: loose fitting in the country style, but the fabric was so fine and the print so delicate, like a waterfall dotted with pebbles. It was unlike anything I'd ever seen before.

The photographer had me sit on the lower level with my legs crossed, looking over my shoulder. There were models in some of the ladies' magazines left at the train station or in the employment bureau waiting room. Those girls in the magazines made it look so easy, but now with the lens pointing at me, I didn't know quite what I should do.

"No, no, no!" cried the photographer in the end, throwing the cover from his back. "I know I said 'less racy' but you're not in church now!" He pulled up my dress on one side to reveal my stocking top and before I knew what he was doing he slid his hand around my thigh and gave it a squeeze. I stiffened. It was all I could do not to slap his face for him. My cheeks were burning as he loosened his grip and I turned my eyes to the floor. I couldn't help but think of Leon and the way he squeezed me and kissed the inside of my thighs as I writhed and gasped on his bed. I threw my head up, full of indignation.

"Tomorrow, make sure you shave above the knee," he said. The other girls giggled and covered their mouths.

At the close of the day none of them waited for me, but I saw Livia and Neomi in a bar just off Mariahilfer Strasse as I made my way back to my room. They were with a few of the other girls, laughing and drinking some kind of cocktail which was served in a funnel-shaped glass with an olive at the bottom. There was a platter of *hors d'oeuvres* on their table and two silver ashtrays which a waiter was emptying. I sighed and walked on, back to that towering building with its dirty windows and its railings with their blistered paintwork. I doubted I'd ever call it home.

"Fourteen?" asked Jonas Lehner holding out the key. There was no vivacity about him whatsoever now he was alone. It was as if the man I'd seen on that first night had died. As I took the key, he didn't look up from his article – something to do with the Montenegro conquest.

I was bored with this war. I flopped into bed still in my blouse, hoping the photographer wouldn't touch me again in the morning. I thought of Leon and I inspected the hairs on my thighs. They seemed sparse enough to me, although they were dark, I supposed. I wondered whether he'd minded too much – Leon – and I found myself wondering too about Giselle and whether she would have sugared her legs or armpits in the American style. No, there was even more of the countryside in her than there was in me. She was probably pickling cabbages and bottling beetroot ready for winter already, darning Leon's socks and helping her father with the farm. Her eyebrows were thick – I tried to picture her face. No, there was nothing sophisticated or citified about her in the least.

When I woke up, my room was pitch black. I could hear Neomi and Livia laughing in the corridor and a loud clang as one of them dropped something.

"Ladies!" I heard Herr Auer booming. "The rent, please. I shan't ask you again."

I heard one of the girls let out a long "Shhhhhh," and imagined Livia standing there with her blonde hair all tousled and her finger on her lips. Then they were both laughing again and I heard the clatter of their heels as they ran off up the stairs.

"Shhhh, Herr Auer," continued Livia. "You know you can't stay mad at us for long!"

Their door banged and there was the sound of muffled chatter. They were in the room directly above mine. I hadn't realised. As I lay awake in the darkness, the grandfather clock chimed in the hallway. It was past midnight. At length, their chatter subsided, but soon afterwards, in tempo with the swinging pendulum, I was sure I heard the creaking of their bedsprings. At first I convinced myself I must have been wrong, but then came the unmistakable sighing and moaning, and I could just make out Livia's voice. She used all kinds of improper language; the shock of it made me quite hot. I got out of bed and threw open the window, hoping the sounds from the street below might drown it out. But as I lay back down and pulled the blankets over my shoulder against the cold, I found I couldn't help but think of Leon and of how he made me make those same sounds when we were on our own in his room, when he stroked the inside of my thighs, when he kissed my belly and made me arch my back. But then he'd press himself urgently against me and I'd have to tell him to stop, and all I could think of were his brothers and what they did to me, even though I kicked and scratched and begged them not to do it.

Outside, there was little noise to distract me; only spasmodically, the humming of an engine and the musical chiming of glass against the pavement – most probably a stray cat knocking over a milk bottle onto the cobbles. Upstairs the creaking bed grew more frantic and Livia squealed and swore so loudly, as if she cared nothing for who might hear her.

I couldn't help it: I touched myself. I held my breath and hoped nobody could hear me. I thought of Leon and of how if I could have just one more chance with him he might make me cry out like that, and how this time I wouldn't tell him to stop.

Chapter Two

I slept in late and woke up to the sound of them knocking at my door again, and when I opened it bleary-eyed in my clothes crumpled with sleep, there they were – Livia and Neomi, bright as buttons. I wondered if they knew I'd heard them last night. I wondered whether they knew how much I liked it, and quickly tried to shut the thought from my mind.

Neomi wore a silver clip in her fringe, with a little square of glass framed with small diamantés, which was quite striking against her black tresses. Her hair was shiny and sleek; she didn't look as severe as before.

Livia was drawing on a cigarette. Wisps of grey smoke curled their way into my room, filling the air with the same unpleasant smell which hung on her breath and in her clothes, even over the scent of her perfume, which was strong and oriental. "Sorry to trouble you again, Selina, but do you have any coffee? We've quite run out, haven't we, Neomi? And the rent...well, let's just say it's more pressing... Sorry."

"Of course," I replied, but all I could think of was my jar with my coffee grinds mixed with chicory. It wouldn't last me the week.

"Perhaps you might like to join us for drinks afterwards?" she continued.

I could scarcely hide my pleasure, for I had not a single friend in the city. Vienna was a bleak and characterless place, I was beginning to consider. The solitude of my stark little room was ebbing away at my initial drive to succeed.

Neomi asked me whether I'd be going to the studios again that morning and whether they could share my cab. "Here, have a cigarette," she said, pressing it into my hand with a book of matches. I tried to give it back to her but she would hear none of it. "Save it for later if you don't want it now."

I thought of the last few Kronen in my purse. "I might walk," I told her. "People say the only way to see Vienna is on foot." I couldn't tell whether they were amused or annoyed.

Neomi and Livia caught the tram in the end, and I walked to the studio as I'd planned. But the sky was so grey and ominous, I wished I hadn't. The clouds loomed dark as widows' sables and the city looked quite ugly as they tightened. There was a loud clap of thunder, the heavens seemed to split open and rain came lashing down against the pavement. A passing motorcar splashed dirty water all up my stockings and around the hem of my coat. The driver held up his hand to me by way of apology. My hair was drenched and stuck to my neck and sides of my face like rats' tails.

When I arrived at the studio I was filthy and bedraggled. Fräulein Flöge surveyed me for a moment. She took me into her office.

"Selina," she said, "I have been very impressed with your attitude, but..." She had a kind face; a broad, handsome face with brown hair which kinked out as it willed, and skin and eyes which were dark like mine. "You are still very inexperienced; the photographer tells me he is having to do a lot of work with you in order to bring you up to scratch. I have an associate, a painter," she lowered her voice. "You may have heard of him – Gustav Klimt." She took a catalogue from her desk drawer and showed me some of his landscapes: *Malcesine on Lake Garda* with its gaily painted Veronese pensions which rose out of the hyacinth-coloured waters and ascended away towards the battlements; his *Farm Garden with Sunflowers*, a delicate symphony of florae, scattered with the most fragile of little wild flowers, which seemed to scream out unashamedly in shades of ruby and sapphire and was bursting with sunshine. But there were the other paintings. *The Marsh*, dead and brown, and the shadowy *Fir Forest* with its narrow trunks, like prison bars, which drew the eye into a frightening, murky place. I thought he must have had a depth to him which would be very dark indeed.

"He paints women too," she told me. I didn't know why I should have been surprised. "Beautiful women. Even when he isn't painting them he surrounds himself by them. He likes them to be naked; it is all very tasteful. I thought you might like to model for him; it would be a great honour for you, Selina."

I felt shocked, flattered she thought me beautiful enough but shocked all the same. "What will I have to do?"

"Just take off your clothes and let him look at you." She shrugged, as if the idea of it didn't faze her at all. I felt my neck and shoulders grow hot. "You will be paid, of course. I shall get you a cab after you have dried yourself off."

The studio was situated at the top of a suite of rooms. I flung open the doors, not expecting to find so many people within. Inside, it was smart with a polished oak floor and huge rectangular windows offering a panoramic view over the city. The chatter stopped abruptly and it was as if all eyes were on me. I was suddenly conscious of my fusty overcoat with its splashes of mud, and my stiffened collar, which had crumpled in the rain.

"Selina Brunner," I announced, although I didn't know which one of them I should be addressing. One of Klimt's assistants directed me behind a screen of cream damask and handed me a robe. I felt myself tremble and my neck grow stiff, and it was all I could do to unbutton my blouse and release the clasp of my brassiere. I stood there for several minutes with it hanging loosely from me; it was only as I began to hear the tutting and sighing from the room outside that I reached for the gown which I had flung over the top of the screen.

There was a padded window-seat, upholstered in red. It was here she told me to sit – the assistant who was slender and whose hair was blonde and scraped back into a bun. She unrobed me as if I was made of marble rather than flesh and I cringed at the peeling of the gown. She turned my face towards the sun and arranged my limbs with one leg bent at the knee, my foot resting on the cushion and the other leg stretched out towards the floor. She eyed me steadily and I tried to hide my shame. I resisted the urge to cover myself with my hands. It was an unnerving feeling, being stared at so openly; I did not know how I should be. There were other women too, all of whom were arranged statuesquely, but we were not to be his muses: that honour lay squarely with Janika Mayer. Janika was beautiful, with auburn hair, which hung long and rippling, high, wide cheekbones, and cat-like eyes – cool grey eyes, but sharp and arresting none the less.

She addressed the maestro, who was the only male in our company. He was a handsome enough man, with the physique of a master builder rather than an artist, and a neck as strong as a bull's. But he was old, in his fifties and balding, his remaining hair fuzzy and coarse. I looked at his colourless smock and his hard, tanned face. He was not as I expected.

"Where do you want me, Gustav?" she asked. There was no nervousness about her. She smiled – only a little smile, for her mouth was small like a bud.

He didn't speak, only glanced briefly at a chaise longue in the centre of the big room, which was shrouded in white silk. It was the silent language of lovers, I thought. He took off her robe and she sat down obediently, reclining with the soles of her feet pressed together and her lovely heart-shaped face thrown backwards. We could see all of her: her breasts, which were firm and white, the curve of her waist and of her belly, sloping down towards the mound of soft chestnut hair. The whole of her womanhood was on show like a red calla lily, which he had her tease and stroke gently. The whole room was silent but for her little gasps and sighs.

Klimt himself, though, did not seem voyeuristic in the least. This was no grubby peep show; he looked at her intently for a while and lifted up his brush and let it dance upon the canvas. His brushstrokes at first seemed loose and easy, but there was a kind of method to his work. I'd never seen such concentration. He focused only upon his muse and his painting which was opening out like a bright flower before him. The rest of us were only on the periphery for him, it seemed, simply particles in an atmosphere which he soaked up and channelled into his art.

The tension in the room was palpable, and I sat there rigidly with my own arousal rising but decorum preventing me from succumbing to it. Finally, Janika was caught in a wave of ecstasy and her body moved rhythmically as she yielded to her climax.

I stood up quickly, put on my robe, snatched up my clothes and ran from the room, down the rear staircase and out into a little enclosed courtyard, around which the building seemed to have been constructed. The ground was still shining with the morning's rain but the sky had brightened a bit. What was I doing here? I was nothing like these Viennese ladies with their avant-garde manners and lax morals. It would be very difficult indeed to find a woman with such low standards back in Tyrol, I was certain.

I sat down upon a bench beside a magnolia tree, pulling my robe more tightly around myself. Shakily, I rummaged inside my purse for the cigarette Neomi had given me and lit it with a match which I threw away into a pot of crocuses standing just to my left. Its taste was less unpleasant this time and I didn't choke, except when I breathed it deep into my lungs. Perhaps it might be better just to hold the smoke for a moment or two in my mouth, I decided, or at most draw it just a little way back into my throat. I hadn't even considered Fräulein Flöge, or my precarious finances. I heard the tread of high-heeled shoes on the fire escape inside the building. I didn't know what I should do next.

The doors behind me opened fully and a woman stepped out. It was Janika Mayer, making her way out onto the courtyard, her face still glowing. She sat down beside me and lit a cigarette. "Are you alright?" she asked.

I nodded. "Yes… Sorry. It's my first time in the city, and I've never done anything like this before. Vienna isn't as I imagined it… I came here as a fashion model."

She put her hand on mine. "Vienna can be a very lonely place," she said. "Will you come for coffee with me?" She was so celebrated within the bohemian circle and I, merely a bumpkin from Tyrol. I could scarcely believe she was talking to me.

"I'd like that," I replied.

She gave a little laugh. "Perhaps you should get dressed first!"

We walked along a broad avenue lined with hazel trees, past the opera house and the City Hall, and turned up a narrow side street in which nestled a bustling coffee house owned by Frau Böhm. The doorway opened out into a spacious room, bright in the centre with darker recesses where men sat reading their newspapers and debating loudly on matters of politics and art. Journalists and essay writers worked alone at tables though the salon didn't have any air of loneliness about it. It was a place of fleeting movement, of social encounters. There was something quite subversive about the whole ambiance, though I knew not what.

"Coffee?" asked Frau Böhm.

Janika nodded and the lady scribbled in a notebook, tore off a little rectangle of white paper, folded it neatly and placed it upon the table.

Janika asked me all about Tyrol, what I'd done there and how I'd managed to secure myself a place at the salon, whether I had any brothers and sisters and what my family home was like. She let me talk to her, nodding graciously until the conversation ran dry and we hit a wall of silence. We sat there for some moments, both looking at each other, at a loss for what to say.

Eventually, I laughed – only out of nervousness, but it seemed to cut through the tension like a blade.

"You look as if you wish to ask me something, Selina."

Janika's smile was one of mischief. I was silent again for a while. "As if you're curious as to how I could have sat in the studio and done...done *that* today."

"I did wonder," I admitted. "I'm not judging you; in fact, I thought it incredibly brave."

"We're all part of the rich fabric which is making up this culture of unsurpassed excellence. It's so exciting! Art is becoming more and more feminine, do you not think? It's so rousing to be able to express ourselves! And what can be more expressive than the act of self-love? It's so unashamedly liberating! Tell me, did it arouse you, Selina? Only it looked to me as if you were quite aroused. Indeed you seem still to be so. It is a terrible thing is it not, the ache of—"

"Coffee!" Frau Böhm's voice came sharply as she placed our drinks before us, with a small jug filled with cream, and a matching sugar bowl with silver tongs.

"Thank you." Janika picked up a lump of brown sugar and dropped it delicately into her cup. I was glad of the intrusion. "Anyway," she continued, "I could ask you the same thing, Selina. What would make a bright young woman take off all her clothes and sit there naked just to satisfy an old man's whim?"

"I needed the money," I said quietly, thinking of my room. At least the coffee house was warm. She'd noticed my missing button, I was sure, but she looked away. As I relaxed a little and took in my surroundings I could see there were others like me, with frayed hems and laddered stockings, although the confidence they exuded rendered their shabbiness almost invisible.

"We never do anything solely for money." She sipped at her coffee. "Tell me, Selina, what was the real reason? Curiosity? Vanity? Ha!" she cried as I threw up my head. "You're a haughty one! Why don't you take me to your room?" I looked at her, taken aback by her forwardness, but she just shrugged and bit her lip. "Why don't you?"

We rushed back there at such a pace that I felt quite breathless and giddy, past the photographer's studios and up the side street where I'd arranged to meet Neomi and Livia. I thought as we approached it that I should pop into the bar quickly, make my apologies and tell them I'd committed to a prior engagement, which had quite slipped my mind until now. But as I looked in through the blinds, I could see the place was empty but for a young man who was propped against a stool at the bar drinking beer. I presumed him to have been a soldier because one of his legs had been amputated just below the knee. It didn't matter to me anymore that Neomi and Livia weren't there to meet me; the only thing compelling me was the urge to get back to my room. We hurried along the cobbles behind my boarding house, towards the back entrance where newspapers lay sodden in the gutter. I thought I might kiss her there – I was dying to do it, in fact – but there was a sweeper in the alley and a man wearing a business suit was just leaving the adjacent building. Finally, we reached the back staircase and I bolted up towards my room with an urgency that made me ache. We reached my door and I fumbled with my key in the lock until at last it yielded and we fell into my room. Then Janika grasped me by the back of my hair and crushed her lips against mine. I gasped with relief and pressed myself up against her. She pushed me down on my bed and pulled my blouse from out of my skirt, undoing my brassiere, pushing it up. I clung to her, desperately with my legs shaking, moving in time with her touch. But all at once I didn't know what was happening anymore and I was fighting her like a tiger in a cage.

"I'm sorry!" she put her hand to her face as if reviled by herself. "Selina, I didn't mean to hurt you, I'm sorry."

"It isn't you," I whispered. Tears sprang to my eyes and I couldn't even bear to look at her.

She held my hand and she stroked my hair until I rested my head against her shoulder. "Did somebody do something to you?" she asked in almost a whisper. "Has somebody hurt you?"

I nodded; I couldn't stop, and I felt the tears spilling out. I was weeping and she was stroking my hair, soothing me, making it all better. But I was crying not only for that; I was crying for Tyrol. I was crying for the loneliness that had swallowed me up since coming here; for Leon who I loved and was gone from me forever…and for the blessing of safe, human touch.

"Yes," I said at last. I said it so quietly, I couldn't quite believe I'd finally said it. I'd set myself free. "Yes," I cried louder. "Yes…when I lived in the countryside." I broke into sobs and let her comfort me until at last my tears ran dry. My head hurt and my eyes were raw.

"Who did this to you?"

I sighed. "I had a friend," I said, "in Tyrol. A boy, his name was Leon."

She nodded for me to go on. "What was he like?" she asked.

"He was handsome." I tried to recall his face, dark with those warm eyes which none of the girls in the village seemed able to resist. "Everybody liked him; I've known him since we were children. He lived on the next farm – his family grew crops and kept a few goats, but times grew hard after the war began and his father sent him to work in the salt factory. It made a man of him. He was tired most evenings, after he'd finished work. I used to go and rub his shoulders for him, draw his bath and shave him. I'd finished school by then and I was helping my mother out in the farm kitchen. We used to sell produce to the shops in town. I'd never gone all the way with him. I wouldn't. Not unless I was sure he was going to marry me. Then, one day, I went to his house after the factory had shut but when I got there he wasn't in, and his brothers who I hardly knew – they were older, I'd seen them around the village many times – they said I could come in and wait for him…but it was all a trick…" I heard my voice tail off.

I could remember standing at the front door. There was a bicycle abandoned beside the path. It had been there so long that weeds sprang up between its spokes. The cottage didn't have window boxes or flowers in the yard like my own. Leon's mother was dead; the place was in need of a woman's touch. When the door closed behind me they were both there: Luca and Elias who were men already. Luca exposed himself to me and Elias ordered me to take off my blouse. My hands were shaking so much I couldn't undo my buttons and in the end they tore it off me.

"And I'm so angry, Janika!" I was shouting. They had no right!

My tears welled up again and I could hear myself whimpering like an animal. Janika was silent for a while. "What did they do to you?" she asked me finally.

Did it matter? All that mattered to me was the way I felt, the way I felt when their stench was all over me and I couldn't wash myself clean because bath night wasn't until Sunday, and it was only Thursday so I couldn't get rid of the horrible sticky feeling. The fear never left me. It seized me sometimes at night and forced itself into my mouth, stuffed itself into my body until it choked me. That was the only thing that mattered to me.

It was as if Janika didn't know what she should do. She kissed me again, but she seemed reticent, far more gentle this time as she curled her hand around the back of my neck and caressed it lightly. She slid her hand up my thigh again, and I drew back from her, looked into her eyes which were calm and pale.

"It's alright, Selina," she said. She drew me to her and kissed me again and I felt her hand pushing the silk of my knickers to one side. I heard Livia and Neomi returning drunk from wherever it was they'd gone to after work, laughing and staggering along the corridor, then Janika was pushing at me gently.

I gasped.

"It's not so bad, is it, Selina?" she asked, but I felt myself start to stiffen against her. "Shhh, Selina, it's not so bad, it's not so bad," she kept saying. "Just love me, everything is alright." I felt the tension drain from my body. I wrapped my arm around her waist as her lips fluttered against my neck. I felt her stroking me, and heard myself moaning. I couldn't have stopped myself even if I'd wanted to.

Chapter Three

I woke before her to the chorus of rose-finches. Her dress lay crumpled on my bare floor; I picked it up and held it to my cheek to feel its silkiness against my skin. It was exquisite. The fabric looked as if it had been designed by Klimt, ivory with an abstract print of flowers: roses and bluebells and gerberas in glorious shades of violet and topaz and gold, but it was shapeless and hung loosely on Janika like an ill-fitting nightgown.

I laid out some eggs, bread rolls, a pat of butter and a few slices of meat, ready for when Janika woke up, but she showed no signs of stirring. I gazed out through my window at the people who looked like toy figurines on the pavement below, watching them go about their day. At first, there were only one or two, but after a while, the street seemed busier and there was the odd bicycle and the hum of an engine.

"Good morning, Selina," Janika sighed sleepily. I wished she hadn't woken; she'd lain there making soft noises of contentment and she looked so beautiful with her eyes shut and her hair fanning out around her face like a halo.

I smiled at her. "I've put out some breakfast." I turned my eyes proudly to the little table. She put her underwear back on, and picked up a cardigan which was hanging on my bedstead, poured herself some orange juice and helped herself to bread.

"The bacon's good," I told her.

"I'm Jewish," she replied. I flushed at my thoughtlessness, but her smile persuaded me it was alright. She might have even liked my naiveté, I thought. "Most of Herr Klimt's ladies are."

"Janika…" I began. Outside, I saw a dove soaring, floating on the morning breeze, higher and higher, gliding wherever the wind took it. I felt such a rush of freedom, I wanted to say something, tell her what a wonderful thing she'd done for me. But my thoughts were interrupted by a loud knock at the door – Neomi and Livia looking tired and wanting their coffee, which seemed to have become somewhat of a routine these last mornings.

"I'm afraid Selina and I have drunk the last of the coffee," said Janika tightly. "Perhaps you two ladies could take yourself off to a little coffee shop somewhere? There are plenty of them in the city."

The two of them stood there not speaking. Janika stared at them more intently and let her cardigan fall open to reveal her cream camisole and knickers. I could make out the curve of her breasts.

"Perhaps we will, won't we, Neomi?" Livia smiled with her same old false smile. "We were merely trying to be friendly, we're sorry to have intruded. We shan't call in on you so often, Selina."

Janika only nodded in condescension. "I shouldn't like to see them take advantage of you," she said to me once they'd gone. I sat down beside her at the table. She took a lock of my hair and wound it absently between her fingers. She brushed my cheek gently with the back of her hand and lifted up my chin so that my eyes met hers. "This is Vienna – there are bad people everywhere. Let me look after you, Selina. I won't let anyone hurt you, not ever again."

I rested my head on her shoulder. That was what I needed, more than anything: a protector in this city where nobody cared about anyone and everyone was out for what they could get.

I hoped she might stay longer but after she'd eaten she slipped on her dress and picked up her bag. "I'm sitting for Klimt again today."

"Shall I come with you?" I asked.

"Not unless he's particularly asked for you." She kissed me and made her way out onto the landing. I heard her footsteps echo away down the stairs.

I didn't know what to do. I went down to the newspaper shop and bought myself a packet of cigarettes and a book of matches, went back to my room and smoked two of them in succession; they made me feel giddy and light, so much so that I needed to lie down for a while on my bed. I could see the breakfast dishes still there on the table, the plate of meat hardly touched, Janika's cup of coffee half-drunk with her lipstick smudged around the rim, and the crumbs left over from her bread scattered over her plate. I looked at them blankly, feeling no impulse to get up and clear them away. All at once nothing seemed dirty any more. I closed my eyes and gave way to sleep.

Klimt didn't ask for me, and neither did Fräulein Flöge. Neomi and Livia didn't even speak to me when they passed me on the stairs, but I heard them most nights making love in their room. Janika visited me most evenings but the days seemed terribly long. I wrote letters to my family in Tyrol, went to see exhibitions at the gallery and the Wien Museum on Karlsplatz, anywhere that was warm, where admission was free and I could at least improve my mind while my days were idle. But my purse was soon empty; I was short on the rent that month and increasingly frequented the library and the park so as to avoid my landlord as well as I could.

I knew there was no escaping it: one evening, quite late, there was a knock at my door. I hoped it would be Janika and rushed to greet her in just my gown. It was Herr Auer. I tried to hide my disappointment and held my gown tightly across my breasts.

"May I speak with you, Fräulein Brunner?" he asked. I could smell *Schnaps* on his breath and the pomade in his hair. His buttonholes heaved with the heavy rise and fall of his ribcage. "Your rent is overdue." He was standing so close to me that I had to step back. He came into my room and closed the door behind him. "Do you have it for me?"

"I'm a few Kronen light, Herr Auer," I admitted,

lowering my eyes. How foolish I was! I thought I'd make my fortune in Vienna and go back to Tyrol in the summer with a trunk filled with new dresses and French perfume. "Could I have a little more time, please?"

He took my hand and pressed it. It was all I could do not to snatch it away. His skin was clammy and hot, the touch of him repelled me.

"There are a lot of girls wanting rooms in the city," he told me, "and it's not good business sense for me to turn them away in favour of guests who can't pay. Perhaps you could consider sharing your room? Only with another girl of course…although I realise there's not much privacy here… You might have to share a bed even." As he uttered those words his face grew purple and beads of sweat erupted from his forehead. "Forgive me," he said, wiping his brow with his free hand. "I don't wish to tell you what to do. Perhaps we could come to some kind of private arrangement?" He looked down at his groin and all I could think of was Luca when he'd ripped open his fly.

I felt the old panic rising in my throat. "I have some jewellery! A necklace, from my gentleman-friend in Tyrol." I felt it beneath the fabric of my gown. "I shall sell it right away, Herr Auer."

"Let me see," he said, and moved my robe aside to inspect the pearl which nestled between my breasts. He looked pleased with himself and nodded. "Goodnight, Selina. I'll expect to see you in the morning."

I rushed to the washstand and began scrubbing his sweat from my skin with the orange-oil soap my mother had given to me as a gift. I could smell the sweet scent of it as I lathered the palms of my hands and washed between my fingers and down the side of my thumbs. I took my nail brush and scoured the feel of him from me. Remembering my pearl, I frantically pulled at the clasp to my necklace and threw it into the basin. I took up my nailbrush again and started scraping the patch of skin where it had lain between my breasts, harder and harder until its bristles were red with my blood. It was only then that I threw the brush from me in abhorrence and clutched my towel to my chest, nursing my injuries and crying for the shame of what I'd done.

Chapter Four

I took my necklace to Levines', the Jewish pawnbroker on Bundesstrasse. A bell rang shrilly as I entered and a man of perhaps fifty appeared from behind a curtain at the rear of the shop. It was a higgledy-piggledy place whose shelves were heaving with curios: fur cravats and muffs, pewter ornaments, bits of brass and old war medals. There was a glass coffer where the jewellery was kept.

I took my silver necklace from my purse. Leon had put a deposit down on it and paid a little every week until finally the account was paid off. The pawnbroker inspected the hallmark through his monocular and weighed the chain on a set of balances.

"Very pretty," he said, turning the small pearl over in his hand. He was a tall slender man with well-groomed hair which had mostly turned to grey. When he smiled, I could see his gums had receded a little and his teeth looked loose in his mouth. He offered me a few Kronen for my necklace. It was enough to cover that week's rent at least, but not as much as I'd hoped. I promised myself I'd buy it back before the twelve months' holding period was up, although I had no idea how I might pay my rent the following week, or the week after that, or any other week for that matter.

In the end, I was forced to swallow my pride before making my way back to the salon.

"Do you have any more modelling work for me, Fräulein Flöge?" I asked.

She looked ill at ease. "I am afraid not, Selina. You were not quite what we were looking for." I turned away. I would have to vacate my rooms; I had no means of supporting myself. "Gustav told me you left his studio before the painting was complete. I recommended you in good faith."

I felt the tears stinging my eyes. "I apologise, Fräulein Flöge."

"You embarrassed me, Selina."

"I know," I said, "and I'm sorry. I appreciate the opportunity you've given me, really I do, and I'm sorry to have let you down. Only, now I can't pay my rent and my landlord... I'll do anything! I can't go back home."

Fräulein Flöge put out her hand as if to touch me but then quickly drew it away. "Perhaps front of house?" she said at length, almost as if talking to herself. "I think a girl like you will be in keeping with the salon's image. Can you wait on customers, be discreet...courteous at all times? These things are fundamental to the success of Schwestern Flöge."

I nodded. It was hardly what I had in mind when I boarded the train from Tyrol.

Fräulein Flöge was a formidable woman: a business woman and couturier. Her salon at Mariahilfer Strasse was the leading fashion venue for the idle ladies of Viennese society. There was a stark atmosphere to the salon with its white walls and square lines. A huge rectangular mirror rose up from floor to ceiling, and the windows were shrouded only in a thin silk curtain that softened the light. Everything was geometric: the high-backed chairs and the square coffee table with its glass top and vase of snowdrops in the centre, the hexagonal mirrors on the wall. It was an apt background indeed for the provocatively bright clothes that hung on mannequins, accessorised with strings of beads and drawstring purses. A huge display cabinet all in silver housed the jewellery, shoes and millinery – not too over-stocked, just a few tasteful items placed strategically. There was a brooch in particular, very art nouveau, which caught my eye – gilt square set around the edges with coral, opal and lapis lazuli, the type of thing I imagined I might purchase with my first month's wages in Vienna, and take with me, pinned to my coat as I went back to Tyrol in style. My ambitions had been reined in, shall we say.

"Make them feel beautiful," said Fräulein Flöge, "and the sale is almost made. There is beauty in all women. All we have to do is tease it out, instil in them a confidence and their beauty will come radiating out like a bright light." I thought of Janika all those weeks ago in the studio with her womanhood on show for us all to see, and felt myself redden. Fräulein Flöge's mouth twisted into an inscrutable little smile; she was a serenely quiet woman, with immeasurable focus. As the days went by, she worked at the tailor's dummy like a sculptress, with a row of pins pressed between her lips, at intervals removing one, tucking it into the fabric and replacing it with another.

"Oh, good morning, Sophia!" Fräulein Flöge seemed brightened as her French patron, Madame Poiret, swept into the salon with her maid trailing behind her. "You look to be in exceedingly good health if I may be so bold." I looked incredulously at the lady who was puffy and bloated and whose brow glistened with tiny pearls of sweat. "Are you looking for anything particular today or just browsing?"

Browsing! I soon learned that women often came into the shop with the sole intent on looking at the dresses and feeling the fine cloth between their fingers. A dress from Schwestern Flöge cost four times as much easily as those in the new department stores. Our custom was more few and far between, but that was the nature of the clothes; they were more exclusive and the clientele more select.

Madame Poiret beamed proudly. "My daughter has announced her wedding; I am looking for an outfit for myself, something in powder blue."

I stifled a smile. "Perhaps something in more of a petrol colour," I suggested, "or indigo. Pastel colours can be very draining for a more mature lady."

Fräulein Flöge dropped a corsage she'd been pinning to a jacket.

"Selina!" she snapped. "Apologies, Sophia, she is new... and very young... Do take a seat, please. Selina! Coffee."

She led the lady over to the glass table. In the coming days, I would come to see it as a place where accounts were drawn up and customers courted.

"We have some beautiful fabric," I could hear Fräulein Flöge saying, "in sapphire blue, with a lighter thread running through it and some strands of gold to brighten the complexion. I was thinking something with a wide neckline, low enough to show off madame's décolleté."

I brought out the coffee on a tray with a spray of silk flowers. Madame Poiret was nodding thoughtfully. "Or we have some cobalt silk with a white pattern printed on it and some silver embroidery, but I think the sapphire might suit madame better. Selina, bring Madame Poiret a few samples to look at, in blue."

I scurried off to the store room and came back with some rolls of cloth. "Perhaps you might like to look at them in the fitting room?" I asked. I guided her behind the Japanese modesty screen and placed the swatches on the back of an upholstered chair which stood beside a looking glass. I lingered there, not knowing what the etiquette was.

"Selina," said Fräulein Flöge, "take some measurements from Madame Poiret, please. On second thoughts, no, I shall do it myself."

She disappeared behind the screen with her tape measure draped around her neck, and I returned to the shop. A few minutes later, she came back with some numbers scribbled on a piece of paper, and placed it down on the counter. My eyes fell upon the figures: *104, 80, 102.* She snatched up the paper and folded it over, as if the whole thing was none of my concern.

The proceeding days didn't see my aptitude improving. My eye wasn't sharp enough to see which brooch looked best with which dress, or which hat suited a square face, and subtlety completely failed me when a lady with swollen ankles asked to try on a calf length dress.

As soon as the lady left the salon, though, almost as if he had been waiting for her to go, Gustav Klimt appeared in the doorway.

"Gustav!" exclaimed Fräulein Flöge. She left her ledger and breezed into the reception area. Her face was so open and warm as she went to him and kissed him on both cheeks in the French way, but his expression remained flat. He was a closed book, it seemed. "How was Geneva?"

"Good," he said. They looked a handsome pair, somehow, he in his calico suit and she in her fawn coloured gown, loose sleeved and embellished with pink flowers. "Apart from the people. They are half-dead in a haze of absinthe. The sickly stench of it is in every café. There's more of it now than before the ban!"

"This calls for champagne," she said. "Much more civilized! Selina, could you fetch some glasses, please, and a bottle from the cellar?"

He glanced at me when she said my name, but there was no hint of recognition. No doubt, I was one of a hundred girls who had passed through his studio.

I nodded. "Of course, Fräulein Flöge."

As I went away through the lobby, I could hear them laughing about something and when I returned they were sitting at the glass table and he was showing her some sketches – dress designs he'd made. His gowns looked flat, like the cut-outs I used to dress my paper dolls as a child. But they were fantastical, somehow, costume-like with their mosaic of sumptuous colours and their golden whorls. He took the champagne from me and closed his sketch book.

"I've got some tickets for the opera tonight, Emilie," he said.

"Why don't you take Valerie?" There was no harshness in her voice, it was teasing almost.

"Because Valerie's not you." His stare was unwavering. He put down the bottle, took her hand and kissed it. It seemed to me they were more than friends, but I couldn't quite work it out. Fräulein Flöge was such a strong woman that, had the two of them been romantically involved, surely she would have put her foot down against Klimt's intimacies with his models. I imagined he must have thought a lot of her. It is not every day a man rushes back halfway across Europe and takes a woman to the opera. I wondered what the opera was like. I imagined a magical place lit by candelabras, full of expectancy and fervour. The only place Leon had ever taken me was walking through the fields – the same fields I trod nearly every day.

Fräulein Flöge almost looked coy. Then it was as if she'd suddenly remembered I was there.

"Oh, Selina, can you go and see to the display, please?"

They chatted for what seemed an age in the other room, but the display was always so immaculate and so neatly arranged there was little to be done. In the end, I resorted to polishing the glassware and shining the silver until finally Fräulein Flöge came and took my arm gently. "There is only so much polishing you can do."

I hoped the interruption, the diversion of seeing Klimt, and the champagne might have made her forget my shortcomings that day.

"Please don't sack me." I pleaded with her and felt the tears prickling in my eyes. Something made me reach out and stroke her sleeve. She was not an unkind woman; she'd been most patient in fact.

"Can you sew?" she asked. "I am always in need of good seamstresses."

I nodded. Oh, all my dreams! They were crumbling around my feet.

Chapter Five

Fräulein Flöge suggested I take a fortnight's rest before beginning work in the production room. "You look worn out, Selina," she told me.

I decided to go back to Tyrol, just briefly. Fräulein Flöge was right; I was exhausted and had become thin. I couldn't gather the means even to feed myself adequately for the next fortnight.

Janika took me for dinner at Le Truc to bid me farewell. The restaurant was shabby, but its shabbiness only seemed to add to its charm, and the lights were low in any case; the whole place was lit just by candles sticking out of empty wine bottles. I thought how beautiful Janika looked in their flickering glow. The floor was whitewashed and sanded to reveal the wood grain beneath and the furniture was French antique. Various metal wall hangings had been put about the room, enamelled in ivory or cream which had been bashed about over time, revealing the iron-work beneath. The menu was expensive; I was sure the likes of Livia and Neomi could never have afforded to eat in a place such as this. I had whitebait followed by some grilled veal with sage butter and French beans, and drank such quantities of wine I felt quite giddy and could hear myself slurring my words.

"I'll miss you, Janika."

"Ha!" she threw her head back. "I shan't miss you!" She said it so lightly it was as if it was of no consequence at all to her. "I'm so busy at the moment I don't have time to see you much anyway. Klimt's begun a new painting."

"Another one?" I put down my glass and stared into the bottom of it. "Has he finished the last one already?"

She shrugged. "It was only a study. I'm not sure if he'll

ever finish it. This one's different; I think it's been commissioned."

"Sounds exciting," I conceded.

She offered me a cigarette. "Not really; it's quite dull. All day long he has me standing there with my tits on show."

I'd never heard her speak so roughly; it must have been the wine, I supposed. The conversation about the painting was over. She was right, though; our relationship was hardly conducive to work. My bed was so small and we slept so entwined that I often woke in the middle of the night to her kisses and caresses, and it was all so new to me that I was never sated. In the mornings, we were both sleepy and heavy-eyed. More than once I had missed a zero off a customer's bill. It was fortunate they were all so honest, and it was little wonder Fräulein Flöge didn't trust me with the books.

I had chocolate torte for dessert and a sweet liqueur made with almonds, which was so pleasant I ended up ordering a second glass, and a third. My head became quite fuzzy and all miserable thoughts of my new job in the factory melted into a distant haze. Then, in a sudden moment of clarity, I remembered Herr Auer and his rent. "My room!" I blurted out. I'd not made arrangements for the fortnight.

"I'll take care of everything," Janika said quickly. "Don't you worry about a thing." She must have loved me then, I supposed. "I mean, where could we go, Selina, if we didn't have your room? My landlady mixes in the same circles as my parents. Ha! I can just imagine Mother's face now! At least in your room we can make as much noise as we like. I've never heard a girl squeal as loud as you... Except for that slut upstairs, but that one swears and grunts like a man. She must be putting it on, don't you think? I am sure no one could ever make me take leave of myself like that!"

Janika was drunk, she was talking much too loudly. I lowered my head. "I'm sorry," I whispered.

"Sorry? What for? Don't ever apologise for being yourself. I like it... Selina, I know you have been through a lot, but it's all in the past now, isn't it?" She seemed to think she'd somehow cured me, as if the pain of it all had just melted away, as if it was never really there at all. I pushed my chocolate torte around the plate with my fork. I'd left my family behind, run away from everything I knew just to escape from it all, come to this city where women were nothing more than objects wearing high heels and fool's gold. On the nights when I slept alone, I sobbed into my pillow for the shame of what they'd done to me.

"I've never known a girl as easy to please as you before," I think I heard her say. I stopped listening and sat staring at a couple sitting at a table in the corner eating their dinner in silence. I doubted Leon would have agreed with her, though. I doubted it very much indeed. But it played on my mind and, conscious of appearing too eager, when we walked home that evening I made sure not to rush. Instead, we strolled hand in hand with the moonlight shining upon us. As we reached the door, she took a piece of folded cloth from her pocket. "Your silver necklace," she said, and as she opened it, the pearl swung down upon its chain. She put it around my neck and did up the clasp.

Janika made love to me gently like she meant it, and I only sighed and whispered in her ear that I loved her.

And now I was back on the train to Tyrol. Already, Vienna seemed like another world with its coffee shops and artists, naked women, couturiers, bobbed haircuts and reform dresses. The city slipped away and I looked out to the mountains and the pastures which sprawled out around their skirts. There was talk of snipers on the hillside, on the lookout for Italian troops, defending our rivers and towns. The train ambled sleepily through Oberösterreich and Salzburg. I'd only been gone six weeks; the winter was fading away when I left but the springtime had crept along in my absence and everything felt alive. The leaves were still sparse on the trees; some of the buds were yet unfurled, but daffodils and tulips were in full bloom in the cottage gardens and there was blossom in the cherry orchards. I knew that by the time I left again for Vienna there would be bluebells and hyacinths also, the magnolia flowers would have fallen and the branches of the beech trees and sycamores would be heavy with greenery. I was still a country girl at heart.

As we pulled into the station there was a knot of grey cloud in the sky which grew darker and seemed to sink down, almost touching the roof of the salt factory. A man took my elbow to help me disembark and once he'd gone, I rubbed at the place where he'd held my sleeve, as if to expunge his touch from me. I looked up the platform. There was none of the grandeur of Vienna Westbahnhof here, just a hanging basket outside the tea rooms, a large clock having Roman numerals which swung on its hook and a metal sign which read, *Schlossplatz*. That was when I saw him. "Leon!" I shouted. He turned and waved to me. I dropped my suitcase and ran into his arms.

"I've missed you, Selina," he whispered. His complexion which was usually so healthy looked pale. "I got a letter… calling me to the front."

He was little more than a boy! I thought I might be sick.

"Can you not get a job in the mine?' I asked in panic. "With Fabian or your brothers?"

He shook his head and started digging at the dirt with the toe of his shoe. What if I never saw him again?

Leon wasn't much changed. Indeed why should he have been? I'd been gone but a few weeks. He was more muscular, perhaps, but people always said the salt factory was heavy work for a man. I watched him as he carried my case with his other arm held away from his body so as to balance himself. He'd grown strong like a mule.

We walked home through the silver birch forest; past the lake where coots had built their nests, raised up from the water, and stood watching a male bringing twigs in his beak which the female weaved skilfully in with the rest. We shouldn't have lingered there so long; I'd not noticed the storm cloud growing heavier. It burst open and the rain came down so hard that the surface of the lake became choppy and rough. Leon took up my case quickly and we ran to the disused boathouse at the water's edge where ropes lay curled up under the awning and birds sheltered in the rafters. The boathouse smelled damp inside. A flash of lightning illuminated the whole place through gaps in the rotting wood and as the thunder clapped we were plunged into darkness once more. He kissed me there, up against the wall of the boathouse, and all I could hear was the quickening sound of his breathing and the storm raging outside. I did nothing to stop him; it was a shock to me how much I'd missed him. He undid my dress at the back and pulled it down to my waist, with my breasts uncovered and my arms trapped at my sides, but still I didn't protest. I was glad it was like this in fact; glad he was not loving or tender. I didn't love him anymore. The only person I wanted was Janika. I was only doing this for myself, to prove to myself that I could, that I wasn't afraid anymore, that they hadn't beaten me. Then all I could feel was him moving inside me until he at last became still.

"I'm sorry, I'm sorry," he kept saying. The storm had passed over. He drew back from me and helped me do up my dress.

We walked back to the village without speaking. He left me outside my parents' door.

Ours was a farmhouse covered in ivy, with climbing roses on a trellis outside the door and hens wandering freely in the front yard. I crept into the house and walked down the hall into the kitchen.

"Selina!" My mother threw her arms around me when she saw me. I stiffened. "I know you don't like it but I don't care."

"Anyone would think we don't wash in this house the way she carries on!" my father chimed in. He was tinkering with the pump just outside the kitchen door.

My mother didn't answer. She was standing on the quarry tiles in her apron and I could smell the aroma of meat from the range. "You've lost weight, Selina."

"It's those Viennese, Lisbeth, they don't eat; they must think it looks good to be half starved!" shouted my father.

"I've invited your brother and Ilke to dinner, and Leon. He's got himself a job in the copper mine with Fabian, and he's married now, did he tell you?" I felt quite faint.

"They hardly had much choice!" My father came in wiping his hands on an oily rag. "She's pregnant! I don't know what's wrong with young people these days. It's ever since this war started, too many freedoms. You had a lucky escape there, Selina…before things got too far… You know…"

"I thought he was going to the front," I told my father. "Perhaps I misunderstood."

He looked to my mother for help; she gave him that look she so often did when he'd said too much and patted me on the shoulder. "I know you were fond of him, dear. I hope you're not too upset?" I held back tears and shook my head. "Good girl. Your father's right, anyway; there will be far more suitable men in the city. Leon likes the simple life; you'd never have been happy with him. He's far better suited to Giselle."

I went to my room under the pretext that I was tired from the journey and needed to rest before Fabian and Leon arrived with their insipid wives. I sat on my bed and wept silently until all my energy drained away. When at last I could cry no more, I stripped off naked and scrubbed myself at my washstand. Twelve times I emptied the bowl away and brought up fresh water. I got through half a tablet of soap. Still, I couldn't seem to rid myself of his touch.

Mother cooked up some shanks of pork with bread dumplings and Rotkohl, simmered with winter fruits and cinnamon.

My brother made some quip about me needing feeding up. "I bet it's all French or Italian. They think they're too sophisticated for good honest food in the city. Peasant food they call it. Those airs and graces wouldn't get you very far in the country!" He laughed to himself.

His wife laughed too; her belly had grown quite big – it must have been nearly her time. She spoke across me, as if I'd not been there at all. "We were just saying, weren't we, Fabian, how much weight she'd lost. I suppose our figures will be ruined forever, wont they, Giselle, once the babies come?"

"Mine was never as good as Selina's anyway," replied Giselle. She rubbed her belly, although there was nothing very much to see; she must have only been fourteen or fifteen weeks gone at most.

"Well, you'd better keep hold of that waistline anyway, Selina," said my brother, "unless you want to end up a spinster." I looked down and started picking at my meat. He laughed heartily and pointed first at me, then at Leon with his fork. "I always thought you two were going to end up together."

Everyone around the table fell silent. In the end, it was Giselle who broke the tension. She tittered at my brother as if the two of them were old friends. "Oh Fabian, really!"

I imagined the four of them sitting in my mother's kitchen together, the men drinking beer, Giselle and Ilke sitting over a pot of tea and some pastries, chattering on endlessly about babies and pregnancy and their various states of nausea and constipation. "I'm sure there are plenty of men to choose from in Vienna!"

"The young men are all dead from war," Fabian replied. He was right. I doubted he had a single friend left in the village. So many boys, so many of them, all gone. How many more would be lost, and what for? I saw my mother look towards Fabian with tears in her eyes.

Giselle was not to be put off, though. "Have you met anyone, Selina? A nice man in the city, since you've been away?"

I shifted in my seat. She must have forgotten what happened, when she walked in on Luca and Elias, and I was lying on their parlour floor naked from the waist down with my blouse torn open, and blood and grip marks all over my thighs. She'd looked horrified for a second but quickly seemed to collect herself. *'It's her time of the month, leave her alone.'* That was all she could say, and we never spoke of it again, as if it never really happened, although sometimes I caught her looking at me in disgust, especially if I was wearing a new dress or had dressed my hair for something especial, as if the whole thing must have been my fault... As if it was beyond their control. And now she'd married their brother and probably danced with them at her wedding, anything not to rock the boat so that she could be a good little wife to Leon and keep him happy, slip into their family and keep her place at their fireside. Where was this women's movement, this female solidarity I kept hearing so much about? Not here in Tyrol, that was one thing for certain, nor in Vienna where everything – even one's very existence – was a lie.

My mother looked at me expectantly. "Yes," I said at last. "Yes, there is someone, someone back in Vienna."

I saw Leon from the corner of my eye raise his fork to his mouth. He stopped dead in his tracks for a second and his meat fell back down onto his plate.

My mother clapped her hands together. "I knew it, Selina! Why didn't you say anything? Honestly, you never tell me anything about your life; you're so secretive. What's his name? What does he do?"

She had me flustered with all her cooing and fussing.

"Let the girl get a word in edgeways, Lisbeth!" snapped my father, folding up his newspaper and putting it down on the table.

"He's called Jan," I told them. "He's twenty; he is an artist's muse."

"A what?" cried my father. "Doesn't anyone have a proper job anymore? A what? There's a bloody war on! Two thousand dead or maimed last time wasn't there, Lisbeth, at the Isonzo? And the Viennese sit around all day eating pastries and drinking kirsch! Cowards, the lot of them!" He glared pointedly at Fabian, then at Leon and finally his gaze settled upon Giselle's belly. "I hope you're not going to end up in the family way! These young city types are all fly-by-nights, you know, Selina."

"Of course not, Father." I said.

He got up and left the table, took up his tools and went outside to the privy.

All night long, I was restless and troubled by nightmares. I dreamt I was on a train, which ambled slowly along the banks of the Isonzo River, looking out onto the water and the craggy ravine beyond. Then, as I turned my face from the window, I saw my carriage was full of soldiers. The train gathered speed and went hurtling into a tunnel carved into the mountains. We were plunged into a horrible darkness which seemed to open up all around me like a cavern. I could feel fingers on me, at first the gentlest of touches which became mauling, hands pawing at me until I woke up yelling and with my nightgown stuck to my body with sweat. But when I opened eyes, it was even worse. I could see a man, just sitting there at the end of my bed, staring back at me blankly. I tried to move but I was paralysed. I tried to speak but when I put my hand to my mouth it had been stitched up. Then before my eyes he just disintegrated, broke up into fragments and fell to the floor as if he was made of china. I sat bolt upright and my mouth opened wide, gasping in the stale air from my room. I got out of my bed and scrabbled around on the floor, searching for a piece of him, just something I could hold up to prove I wasn't going mad. There was nothing. It must have been a trick of my imagination. I put my hand to my mouth. I crept down to the pantry and came back to my room with a bottle of absinthe, but as I succumbed to sleep I was yet more troubled, thrashing around in what seemed like a state of semi-consciousness until the dawn came.

In the end, I was up with the cockcrow. My room was airy and bright, with a whitewashed floor and gingham curtains. My mother had put a bowl of daffodils in there for me. I crept down to the kitchen, hearing the stairs creak underneath my tread and sat at the window seat looking out onto the walled garden and the coop full of Silkies beyond.

There was a slice of homemade strudel on the kitchen table – Mother again! I'd missed her baking during my time in the city – and some drinking chocolate that I heated up in a pan on the range. She'd got it into her head that it was what we drank in Vienna instead of tea.

In the distance a silhouette of a man appeared, approaching our cottage along the lane. The sun was quite low in the still-yellow sky behind him as he walked beside the bramble bushes and past the abandoned tractor in the field. As he came nearer, his gait was unmistakable. It was Leon, on his way to his work, swinging his bag full of sandwiches at his side. I walked down as far as the gate to meet him. There were carts being pulled along by mules way off in the distance. The lane had become something of a trade route since the onset of war. It was scarred with hoof prints and scattered with salt and crops, spent from passing wagons.

"Selina," he said, not even able to look me in the eye. "I'm sorry. I meant what I said to you yesterday. I've missed you."

I felt the warmth of him as he pulled me to him. "You lied to me, Leon."

"I know," he said, "and I'm sorry. Vienna's made a woman of you."

I nodded, feeling tears spring to my eyes.

"I haven't stopped thinking…about what happened yesterday." He sounded almost as if he pitied me, and when he stepped back from me his expression was grave. "Selina, it should never have happened. I'm married to Giselle. It's too late."

Then as if appearing from nowhere, on the lane there were his brothers, Luca and Elias. Elias tipped his hat to me as if we were old acquaintances and nothing of any consequence had ever happened between us. He said something to Luca and they both laughed.

"Are you alright, Selina?" I heard Leon say.

I turned from him and ran back inside the house.

My mother was standing there in the kitchen, with her

face all sympathetic and her hair tied up in rags. "My beautiful girl," she sighed. I looked at the strudel she'd made me. How terribly disappointed she would be if she knew my glittering future had all come to nothing, or if she harboured any inkling of what I'd done just yesterday in the boat house with a married man, and every night, lying naked in my bed, with a woman, back in my room in Vienna! I couldn't even bear to meet her gaze.

Chapter Six

As planned, I was back in Vienna within the fortnight. I worked in the production room with seventy other women who chattered over the clatter of the sewing machines. There were further tables behind a screen where the pattern cutters sat. I harboured a hope I could make it into the cutting room before too long. I'd heard of factories in London – sweatshops they called them, though according to rumour they were so cold that the nickname was inapt. Women queued outside in the rain and the smog, they said, for hours daily just for the chance of a day's work, but if they failed to make the required number of garments by dinner time they were sent home without a penny in their pockets. At least here, it was the quality of a girl's work that counted, not the number of dresses one could throw together in a day. The room was bright too, and warm, especially now the spring sunshine flooded in through the skylights. Our gaily coloured bobbins kept turning and our needles punched tiny holes through the flowing fabrics. We drank chocolate, we smoked cigarettes in our breaks and we worked on unglamorously. It was a world away from the smart reception area with its glass coffee tables, and a world away from Klimt's studios where Janika went and sat almost daily.

My thoughts settled on her as I stitched the seams of the teal coloured reform dress, and the lukewarm welcome home she'd given me upon my return. When I kissed her she didn't wind her fingers around my neck or rest them in the small of my back as was her way. Instead, she placed her hand limply on my arm, drawing it back after only a few seconds, telling me she'd bought a new blend of coffee for me to try, since I'd written to her complaining that in the countryside we only drank tea and beer. It was smoky, she said, because they roast the beans until they are almost burnt, but not quite. The gesture was thoughtful enough I supposed but as soon as I'd finished my coffee she kissed me on the cheek and said she needed to be up early in the morning.

"You must be tired," she added, "from your journey. I'll let you get some rest."

I dwelt on it as I worked. My thoughts wandered to that first night when I took her to my room, when she'd all but torn off my undergarments, and of the last night together when she ran her tongue down my belly, slowly, agonisingly and kissed me gently until… *Ouch!* I pricked my finger with my needle. Quickly, I put it to my lips and sucked the blood from it.

"A thimble, Fräulein Brunner!" called the supervisor. "Try to be more careful, please!"

I tried for the rest of the day to concentrate on the task in hand but I found more and more that I thought of Janika. I adored her.

She met me sometimes as I left the factory wearily to the sound of the closing bell. Most days there was a stall set out under a banner of *The German Workers' Party in Austria.* They were a collective of men, trade unionists, miners, apprentices and textile workers. They didn't seem to be doing any harm, only handing out leaflets about the rights of workers. There was a man – Rudi Martin from the railway – deep in conversation with one of our seamstresses. All the women knew him; he was big and handsome and there was this little dimple in his cheek when he smiled, which was rare since he was usually so solemn and intense.

"Half of the men on the railroads don't even speak German these days," he was telling her. The observation seemed innocuous enough.

"Fascists!" Janika muttered as she squeezed past him through the crowd of factory women. "They'll be the downfall of us all."

He eyed her up and down, the hem of her silk dress at her calf, the swing of her embroidered purse on her hip as she walked. A pang of jealousy knotted up inside me.

It was over a week before we made love, and even then she didn't kiss me on the mouth, only a little on my neck, and later the backs of my shoulders as I turned away from her feeling empty.

She rolled over, reached for her purse and lit a cigarette. "Klimt's going to unveil the new painting tonight," she told me as she lay on her back, smoking with one arm dangling out of the bed. It was as if she'd only said it to break the silence.

"At least he's completed it – finally!" I returned. I wondered if he'd ever managed to paint over the study he made of her in that most intimate of moments or whether it remained as it was, rough and grainy.

"Will you come? I've bought you a dress."

I looked over to where my few clothes hung on their rail, feeling ashamed of the mended garments, the faded colours and the threadbare elbows.

"I'll have it sent over to you, Selina, and meet you in the studios, say at seven?" She seemed to have the whole thing planned out. "Don't be so grumpy! I'm sick of talking to your back!"

She flung back the covers, put out her cigarette and pulled on her stockings. She was slipping away from me. I was losing her.

A delivery boy brought me my dress that evening, as promised. I saw him approaching on his bicycle from Bundesstrasse with the flat box balanced precariously across his handlebars. The dress itself was not dissimilar to the floral ivory gown Janika had worn on that first day; its design seemed the same though the background was an inky blue. I tried it on over my blouse and stockings, and caught sight of my reflection in the looking glass; it suited me ill. I was a seamstress from Tyrol playing at being a Viennese courtier, that was all. The thought occurred to me I might take off the dress and put on the one my mother made me for Fabian's wedding. I always felt comfortable in that at least. In the end, I stuck with the blue gown as it was more fitting to the occasion.

The studios were bustling that evening with men in worn suits, the type I'd seen before, that day in the coffee house – journalists and critics, I presumed. They all seemed to converse intimately with one another while I stood alone in the dress, brought to me by the delivery boy. A waiter offered me a glass of champagne from a silver tray. I thanked him but as I put it to my lips I felt as if all eyes were upon me, though I suppose they were only looking at the art works. The taste was most unpleasant. In the country, we drank beer, which was yeasty and different entirely.

Janika wasn't there.

The hands on the clock face barely moved. I went to the powder room, I came back, and I took another glass of champagne from the tray. At last, there was the chiming of a dessert fork against a champagne flute. The chatter dwindled away and all eyes were drawn towards the maestro who was standing on a podium beside the window.

"*Death and Life,* gentlemen," announced Klimt and he drew back the satin curtain, unveiling his new masterpiece to much gasping and whispers of "Fantastisch!"

A fawning crowd gathered and there was a drone of flattering comments and sycophantic noise. After some minutes, the throng dissolved, returning to their canapés and drinks. I looked at the painting. The living figures were encased within an arch shape, garlanded with beautiful flowers and printed silks in glorious shades of coral, mint and citrus. To the left of the arch I could see Janika, shrouded in some kind of floral fabric, with her head thrown back and a look of serenity in her eyes. I studied her, with my head tilted to one side and my glass still clutched tightly in my hand. It was indeed Janika, yet changed; more beautiful if that was possible. Her hair was lighter with all the vibrancy of a calendula, her eyes were the coolest grey and her lips like a beautiful wet flower.

She formed part of a circle of life, of women at moments of intense pleasure. My eye wandered around this arch, to the apex where I recognised Neomi, sleeping, with a baby in her arms. She was naked and the white of her flesh was quite striking against the vermillion and tangerine of the drapery upon which she lay. Janika, clothed, was pressed up against her naked body. I held my breath for a second and then, composing myself, I studied the figure of the older lady, her hair covered in a cornflower coloured scarf. One of the other models lay cheek to cheek with the sleeping baby. Beyond the garland of flowers, the canvas was flat and grey; against it was painted the figure of death: a grinning skull draped in midnight-blue cloth decorated with crosses. But rather than cowering from death, the figures seemed indifferent towards it. There was nothing deathly or ugly about the painting; it only depicted incredible beauty and calm.

"Selina!" Janika arrived late, draped all over a tall, dark man with a chiselled face and muscular arms. "Come and meet my friend," she said to him guiding him swiftly towards me. I eyed him with suspicion. He was handsome there was no denying. There was a confidence about him. "Selina, this is my friend, Levi Joel," she said stroking his arm. "He's the male in the painting. It's sublime, don't you think?"

I turned in bewilderment back towards the painting. She laughed. "Why, Selina, you hadn't even noticed he was there! I told you, Levi."

She was right, he wasn't immediately obvious. His dark torso receded against the alabaster flesh of the women; in real life he was neither so dark nor so muscular. It was a painting which celebrated women as life-givers. There was hardly need for him to be there at all.

"Fräulein, excuse me." It was Klimt. I wondered if he remembered at all that I'd posed for him that day in his studio, or that I'd brought him champagne in Fräulein Flöge's salon. He looked older, I thought, since we'd last met. "Word has it that Fräulein Mayer and yourself are... intimate." He fell silent and stroked his beard. I thought we'd been discreet. "I should like to paint your portrait... both of you, as a couple."

I shrugged and felt the old panic rising. My cheeks burned hot and prickly. I couldn't face the thought of it, standing again full-frontal in his studios. I thought of my mother and the sacrifices my family had made so that I might come here, to Vienna where the war and the food shortages in the country were only a distant dream. I couldn't do it.

"Excuse me, Gustav," said Janika. She grabbed my elbow and marched me away, away from all the models and her artistic friends. "What on earth is wrong with you? You shame me! Gustav Klimt has just asked if he can paint your portrait. You could have at least accepted graciously. You're a seamstress, Selina. He is one of the greatest geniuses of our time!"

"Oh, pardon me!" I pulled my arm from her grasp. "But forgive me if I don't feel it an honour to sit there naked for hours on end while an old man stares at my velvet purse!"

"You sound ugly, Selina; you should learn to watch what you say. Klimt doesn't degrade women; he is aroused by women and by painting in equal measure. Why else would he recreate them with such majesty?"

I scrabbled to collect my thoughts. All I wanted was to please her, even though in my heart I knew it wouldn't make her think any better of me. I would have sold away my very soul – anything just to make her happy.

"I'll do it," I said. I couldn't even look at her.

"Oh, don't trouble yourself, Selina!"

But I went with her to the studio anyway. I'd thought it might have been just the three of us this time, but as before, the studio was filled with women in various states of undress. None of them spoke; Klimt asked for silence when he was working, and we were so high up that none of the noise from the Strasse intruded.

When we arrived he had coffee brought for us, and as we sat, he observed us quietly, his face serious and full of composure. He stroked his beard and leaned in towards his assistant.

"That one in the red," he said to her.

She waited for us to finish our coffee and then took me away into a little dressing room, where there were two rails of dresses, some brightly coloured, loud with their swirls and golden prints, others quieter, more formal. There was a mirror propped up against the wall, a great big thing with a frame made entirely from bronze circles, and shelves stacked with props: stuffed animals, bird cages, parasols and Egyptian masks.

He painted us standing side by side, Janika with her head resting on my shoulder. I wore for him a robe of red silk and a white turban and he set us against a background of oriental flowers, surrounded by birds: the glorious phoenix, the raven and the red-eyed swan. She was nude, but for a pair of earrings and some kind of bracelet. His concentration was magical as he gazed upon us, holding up his brush sometimes just before his eyes, as if to measure the length of our necks, or the angle of our hips, or the distance between us. His hands were graceful as he conjured our likenesses out of his palette.

At regular intervals, Klimt took breaks away from his canvas. Often he would disappear into one of the side rooms, where there were yet more women lazing, and close the door behind him. Now and again he took one of them out with him, returning an hour or so later. Occasionally, he would have pastries brought to the studio for all of us, but most of the models ate like birds. It was only during these breaks that he spoke to us, asking me if I was comfortable and not too warm or too cold.

With Janika he chatted more freely. "Have you any plans for the summer?" he asked her.

"I may go to Salzburg for a week. I'm not sure yet." It

was the first I'd heard of it. "And yourself?"

"Lake Attersee again, with the Flöges…for as long as they can stand me, and then back to Geneva if I can. It's a tiresome city, but I have business to attend to there. I much prefer Vienna."

"I should like to visit there one day," said Janika. "I've heard the people are charming."

"When they're not drunk!" He looked almost as if he was about to break into a smile as he said it, but his mouth quickly straightened though his eyes were still lively.

We posed for him that way for weeks until just as I thought it would never end, Klimt laid down his brush and declared, "*The Women Friends!*"

"May we see it?" asked Janika. I'd not seen her so eager in a long time. He inclined his head in assent.

Although I was clothed and she was naked, I was the one who looked uneasy and gauche, imprisoned by my clothes. As for Janika, I never saw her look so contented or as self-assured as she did in that painting.

I excused myself and went to the powder-room where I stood staring into the looking glass on the wall. The portrait was frighteningly accurate; I was as aloof as Klimt had made me. I splashed some cold water on my face and returned to the studio.

"You don't share Fräulein Mayer's enthusiasm?" asked Klimt.

I did my best to muster a smile. "It's exactly as I expected, Herr Klimt."

We walked silently along the avenue, Janika and I, with the sun waning and the shadows growing long.

"You know, Janika," I ventured, "you don't have to do this anymore."

"Do what?"

I stuttered a little. "Take off your clothes for Klimt. You could come and live with me. I know there isn't much room, but it would mean only one lot of rent to pay.

Fräulein Flöge is looking for more seamstresses, business is booming, apparently."

"I'm a model!" she cried, as if it was all a tremendous shock, as if she'd never considered even that there might have been another life. "I enjoy working for Klimt."

I was exasperated by her stubbornness. "Really, Janika, I know you think yourself a bohemian, but what you're doing, it's not real life. You're dishonouring yourself, you're dishonouring me."

She stopped walking and turned around to face me squarely. "You've got the wrong idea about us, Selina. If you want a relationship where one controls the other through sullenness and dark moods, where nothing extraordinary is permitted, where one is locked up in a cage like a twittering canary, if you want all that I suggest you find yourself the nearest man and marry him. I'm a free spirit; I will not be controlled."

She turned on her heels and marched away under the shade of the hazel trees.

Chapter Seven

I imagined it might have been one of those rows that lovers have, a quarrel which could have been fixed by a bunch of flowers and a box of truffles, but a week went by and there was no sign of Janika. I settled back in quickly enough – to the grind of the production room at Schwestern Flöge.

On the first day, there were some comments from the other girls: "How the mighty have fallen!" and "Nice of you to grace us with your presence again, Selina." But I kept my eyes on my machine and they soon seemed to tire of their spite.

By the end of the week, though, I was teary. My heart ached for Janika, just to hear her voice and hold her in my arms again. When the bell sounded at the end of the day, I rushed out past the stall for The German Workers' Party and a girl from the cutting room caught my arm. She was pretty enough, I supposed, but her hair was cropped short, like a boy's.

"Are you not coming to the meeting tonight, Selina?"

I didn't know her name. I shook my head and pushed my way through the crowd.

It was still light as I turned off the square and took a detour from my usual route back to my room, past Frau Böhm's coffee shop where Janika had taken me on that first fateful day. I drew out the spare change from my pocket; there was plenty for a pot of coffee and a pastry, but as I turned towards the door I stopped dead in my tracks. There was Janika with Levi Joel, laughing, holding hands across the table like any other courting couple. I stood watching them through the glass. The cake trolley was brought over to them laden with apple cake, Sachertorte and hazelnut meringues. She looked to him, as if for guidance as to which of the desserts she should order. He smiled and tickled her leg under the table with the tip of his shoe.

"Entschuldigung, Fräulein," said a voice from behind me. I moved aside to let a man into the coffee shop. He went over to a table where a lady sat all by herself. She stood up to kiss him, I lowered my head. Everywhere I looked there was love. I didn't know what I should do. I wandered away and sat myself across the Strasse beside an old lady on a wooden bench. I opened up my purse and pulled out a packet of cigarettes.

I sat there until way past sunset feeling the night become crisp and chill. Vienna was no place for a girl like me; I was drifting here, like one of Klimt's rose petals that had been caught by the passing wind. The old lady had gone. I buttoned up my coat and lit another cigarette. The door to Frau Böhm's shop opened, and out came Janika with Levi Joel. He caught her hand, spun her round and kissed her. I'd never seen her so happy. I despised myself.

I knew I shouldn't have done it, but I couldn't help myself; it was as if I was pulled along after them by some invisible thread. I kept to the shadows, listening to their light laughter and the clip of her heels along Ringstrasse. They looked like a fine couple indeed: Levi wearing an expensive suit, and Janika in her evening gown, draped in a fur stole with her earrings glinting in the glow of the gas lamps. I followed them right down to the doors of the opera house, that beautiful place bathed in moonlight, saw them disappear through one of the monumental archways, watched as the building swallowed them up. I stayed outside for a long time listening to the haunting cry of the violins. I hadn't realised how long I'd been there, but at length the music died away and Levi and Janika were out again in the street. They walked past me, as if I were a ghost. She looked straight through me and Levi shouted down a cab. "Feldstrasse," I heard him say to the driver.

I made my weary way back to my room, alone through the soulless streets of Vienna.

Janika didn't visit me again, but I saw her often. I contrived to see her often, through the window of the little patisserie, in the queue for the theatre, outside Klimt's studio; she was always with Levi Joel, walking with her arm threaded through his and gazing up at him. He must have cast a spell on her, I was sure.

I went back to work on Monday morning in almost a trance. By lunchtime, I'd only made one dress, and even that had a kink in the neckline.

"You'll have to unpick this and start again," said the supervisor. "Is this all you've done, Fräulein Brunner?" She took up a dress from one of the more experienced women to show me as an example. The woman looked at me proudly. "If you are ill, go home! Idleness will not do in this house!"

I could see the other girls looking over at me from the cutting tables. "Sorry," I said, and I began unpicking the stitches.

At lunch time, I barely ate anything, just half a stale pastry left over from the weekend. I went outside into the courtyard and lit a cigarette. It was a stark place, slabbed with slate and enclosed by iron railings with blistered paint. The sky was a blanket of grey; the day was flat.

"There's another meeting tonight, if you'd like to come?" I heard a voice say. It was the girl from the cutting room again with the boyish hair – Anja, she said her name was. Her face was really quite elfin, a perfect oval, and her eyes were big like a fawn's. Only one with such delicate features could have carried off such a haircut, I considered. My face was too long, my nose too aquiline.

"I don't think so, sorry," I replied, and turned my head away.

"I just thought it might be nice," she continued. She laid her hand gently on my arm. "I've watched you ever since you arrived. You're always alone, Selina, and Vienna can be a very cold place." My eyes welled up with tears. "You're not from here, are you?" I shook my head. "Neither am I. I'm from Salzburg. The other girls are nice really once you get to know them, and the boys from the railroad are good fun…though I doubt you have any interest in them." I lowered my head. "Nor do I," she told me. "I'll wait for you when the bell goes."

The meeting took place in the disused Saint Elizabeth of Hungary Chapel. It was a plain enough looking little building from the outside with a low roof and white façade. It lacked some of the baroque madness which seemed to have seized Vienna in its grasp. Inside, the candelabras burned low and the walls were decorated with woodcarvings and a selection of arms.

Behind the altar stood Rudi Martin, the German from the railroad. I hadn't seen such a tall or broad-shouldered man since leaving Tyrol. He took off his cap and held it in his hand. "The German Workers' Party in Austria is not a party solely for labourers; it stands for the interests of every decent and honest enterprise. It is a liberal party, for the people, fighting against all reactionary efforts, clerical, feudal and capitalistic privileges!"

There was much shouting and clapping; the men were loud and riotous, the women uncouth. They jostled each other as they vied for position. The message seemed tolerable enough to me. I was becoming sick of my cupboard being empty, of melting remnants of soap together in tins over a candle just so could have a wash. I hadn't realised it until that moment.

"Before all, we fight against the increasing influence of the Jewish commercial mentality which encroaches upon public life!"

I could no longer hear the racket around me. Everything seemed to be moving in slow motion; the signs of assent, the raised fists.

"We demand the elimination of the Jewish banks!" he shouted.

I needed to get out.

We walked a distance from the building before I turned

to Anja. "Can I invite you for a nightcap?" I asked. The speech had been so provoking, so startling for me that I didn't know myself any more.

I took her to my room down the alley behind the block. I shouldn't have liked Neomi or Livia to bump into her for fear of what they might say to Janika. They were vindictive enough just to tell her out of spite – she might never come back to me. The gutters were still wet from the afternoon's rain and I could hear the water seeping away down the drains. Then, in the dark recess behind the bins I could vaguely make out the shapes of two men, a young man and the other – yes, Jonas Lehner the concierge, with his trousers at half-mast. I felt unclean. I don't know why I should have, it was the shock of it, I supposed, and my upbringing in the countryside where men and women got married, raised a family, went to work and died. My father used to say all kinds of things about men like that, and I heard Leon and my brother making crude jokes sometimes about a boy in the salt factory. I would have to wait a while for my keys that evening, I supposed, and I wondered what I was doing with this girl in this seedy place: a squalid alley behind a shabby block of bedsits.

I went through the motions with her; let her do whatever she wanted to me. When she kissed me, I closed my eyes and thought of Janika. I knew what Janika meant then about being with a girl who was eager and easy to please.

In the end, my eyes grew heavy. I wanted Anja to leave. There didn't seem enough room in my bed for both of us, but she was just lounging there, propped up on her elbow, stroking my hair and gazing at my face. I lay on my back, turned my head away from her and closed my eyes.

I dreamed of Janika, lying naked and covered in flowers, just as Klimt might have painted her.

Chapter Eight

The next time I saw Anja was at the factory gates. I was leaning against the railings, smoking a cigarette with my face turned towards the sun, which was warm with the heat of late spring. She clasped my hands and kissed me on both cheeks, but feeling the bandages underneath my blouse, she drew back in alarm. "Oh Selina! Whatever have you done?"

It was none of her business, this girl who meant nothing to me. "I burnt myself on the cooker," I told her.

"Let me see!" Her eyes were so genuine, so full of concern.

I threw down my cigarette, turned away from her and marched back inside Schwestern Flöge. I was the first one to take my place at my machine that morning. A basket of sleeves and bodices lay at my feet, pinned together, ready to be transformed into the lovely dresses being worn nearly all the time now by well-to-do women on Ringstrasse and in the coffee houses.

It wasn't a burn. I could feel my flesh stinging beneath my dressing. I put my fingers to my eyes and steeled myself against the tears I could feel welling up inside them. I'd left my room that night, walked all the way to Feldstrasse, to the smart row of terraces where Levi Joel lived. What on earth must she have thought of my dingy little room? His was a well-presented house with a red front door flanked by two pillars, set behind a small frontage with a low blue-brick wall, an ornamental bird-bath and window boxes bursting with hyacinths. The candles were still burning in the dining room and the table was set for dinner, but it seemed to have been abandoned. I could see the lid of the piano, gaping open as I peered in through the window, and the wine had been decanted but not yet poured. When I looked up to the first floor windows I saw Janika's silhouette, behind a curtain, naked, kissing him with her hands around his neck as he held her around the waist.

I ran down the hill, through the city, all the way back to my room. I tapped on the counter impatiently as Jonas Lehner turned to fetch my key. All I could think about was getting upstairs, pulling my clothes off and washing the dirt away from me. But as I stood at my wash stand, as hard as I scrubbed I couldn't get clean. My skin was raw, as if it had been flayed, but still I couldn't get it off me. I rushed to the kitchen drawer, pulled out the meat knife and drew it slowly along my arm, feeling the relief of the blood as it seeped out and grew cold against my skin.

When the bell rang for lunch that day, Fräulein Flöge sent a message that she wanted to see me in her office. She was sitting at her desk drinking coffee when I arrived. It was an immaculate looking place with polished bureaus and vases of flowers dotted about the place. The company secretary, Frau Huber, sat at a little table in the corner, upon it a typewriter and photographs of her husband and daughter.

"This is a very delicate matter," Fräulein Flöge said. "One of Gustav's models has complained that you are following her." The shame of it was crushing. "It will not do, Selina. I know you were very fond of Fräulein Mayer but she is to marry Herr Joel and you have to accept it."

I tried to catch my breath. Blood had oozed out from beneath my bandage and stained my blouse. Fräulein Flöge surely must have noticed it but she seemed to be looking at a point far beyond me.

Frau Huber took a sheet of paper from a pile on her desk and began feeding it slowly into her typewriter. She started tapping out a letter; the little bell rang sharply as she reached the end of each line and pushed back the carriage to begin a new one.

"Your work is suffering," Fräulein Flöge continued, "and

this house has a reputation to uphold. Take this as a warning and see that you concentrate from now on."

"I will," I assured her, thinking of my rent and my slithers of soap.

Frau Huber lowered her head. I was sure she was smirking.

"You are a beautiful-looking girl, Selina; I am sure there is a man in Vienna who will make you a good husband. Sometimes it is prudent not to follow your heart."

I nodded. "Yes, Fräulein Flöge."

"It would be better for you if you forget about her."

Frau Huber rapped away at her typewriter until finally she shot up out of her seat. It was as if she could contain herself no longer. "New ribbon!" she said shrilly. She pulled out a packet of cigarettes from her drawer, put them into her handbag and snapped the clasp shut. Frau Huber was a smart looking lady wearing a navy blue skirt and a blouse in cream satin. Her stockings did not appear to have been in need of mending; neither did her shoes, which had a little heel and a bar across the front. She hurried away along the corridor, swinging her bottom and smoothing down her hair. By the time I got out into the courtyard she was already gossiping with some of the factory girls – girls whose names she probably didn't even know, and why they would even entertain her I could not imagine. There were little giggles and looks of shock, then Anja raced away from the others with her hand covering her face.

It was kinder that she knew, I told myself, that she knew that I didn't love her and was in love with somebody else.

Later that day, though, there was yet more scandal. It was all over the factory floor; everyone seemed to forget all about the scene in the courtyard. Fräulein Flöge had received a telegram: Gustav Klimt was gravely ill and was asking for her. She'd sent for her driver immediately, looking white as a sheet. Her best client arrived at three, as arranged but Fräulein Flöge had evidently forgotten all about her.

"They must have been lovers after all, then," remarked

one of the girls. "Why else would he have sent for her?"

Why indeed? A man who was surrounded all day by beautiful women. Fräulein Flöge was different, I'd seen it myself that day in the salon, when they'd drunk champagne and pored over his drawings, when he'd produced two tickets to the opera, assuming she'd accompany him. There was no sense of courtship between them, however, of favour to be won or good impressions to be made. She was his equal, not the kind of woman at all to lie down naked in a room full of people and let him watch her do anything, all in the name of art. The message came back to Frau Huber just before closing time. Fräulein Flöge wasn't expected back until the following week at least, due to the death of a close personal friend.

I don't know why I should have been saddened so. Klimt was merely a wisp in my life, a man whose heart I knew nothing of. Our paths had crossed but a handful of times – he'd probably forgotten all about me the moment he put the last brushstroke on *The Women Friends*. And yet, if I hadn't modelled for him that first time in his studio, Janika and I would never have met. He'd immortalised us together, and for that reason alone I would remember him.

I went home and got drunk on red wine, I smoked too many cigarettes. I lay on my bed and thought only of Janika. I thought of her naked in Klimt's painting, where she looked so lovely, so content with her head resting on my shoulder, the slenderness of her waist, her feline eyes, the pertness of her breasts. I wanted to see it. I wanted to see the painting. But there was no hope of it.

The Women Friends had been sold to a collector who lived just up on the hillside behind Schwestern Flöge. The nearness of it made it even worse; it was so close and yet completely out of my reach. Yet I couldn't forget. I moped around and kept to my room after work. I smoked incessantly and took absinthe most nights before bed, staying up late and thinking constantly about Janika. I didn't know what I should do.

Anja became somewhat of a permanent fixture in my life

but she wasn't the only one. There were a series of meaningless encounters with a string of women, which left me feeling hollow and cheap. I carried on working at Schwestern Flöge and living in my meagre lodgings, and as the years passed I thankfully found that I thought of Janika less and less until in the end, hardly at all...

But one day all that would change.

Chapter Nine

The war raged on still. Soldiers on each side of the line sat in stinking trenches, firing artillery onto the enemy's position and hurling grenades. Each time military leaders ordered a fully-fledged attack, the foot soldiers were forced over the tops of their trenches, running without protection into no-man's-land. The death toll ran into millions; eventually it would be the side with the most men who won the war. Photographs came back of barbed wire twisted around stumps of dead silver birch and of young men's bodies rotting where they lay.

One afternoon in November 1918, Fräulein Flöge came into the production room. The pattern cutters fell quiet and the clatter of the needles petered out. I took my foot off the treadle and looked at her, standing there, wringing her hands as she waited for quiet. It was so rare to see Fräulein Flöge out on the factory floor that I knew the news she brought us must have been important.

"The war is over," she said hoarsely. "Germany has surrendered."

Outside, the sky was grey and still, sleet was hanging on the air. Nobody made a sound for a while. Perhaps my father was right; the war meant nothing to the Viennese. Then one of the girls rushed over to another and hugged her. I heard someone whisper, "At last."

"You may all go home for the rest of the afternoon," said Fräulein Flöge.

I felt this overwhelming urge to go and see my family. There was nothing else to do. I took my necklace back to the pawnbroker on Bundesstrasse. Herr Levine was polishing a silver pepper shaker; his breath had become short and wheezy. "Hello, Fräulein Brunner! The necklace? Let me see."

He unwrapped the pendant from its soft cloth and felt the weight of it in his hand. "Ah." He said it as if the necklace were an old friend. "Shall we say six Kronen?" I was more than happy with the offer. It was ample for my fare with enough left over to feed me for a week.

It was an icy wind that greeted Anja and me back in Tyrol that evening, great squalls that came in swathes from the mountains. There was only a vague impression of their presence – the mountains that soared over the little hamlets; everything I knew had been swallowed up by that blackest of nights. We took the long walk over the beet fields. I could feel the sodden earth beneath my feet. Way off in the distance was the glow of the brazier from the salt factory, bloodying the shadows that lay all around it. From the glow of its flames I could just about make out the squat brick building crammed into the valley. I longed for its warmth. The handle of my carpet bag had broken. I shifted it, first holding it against my chest and then underneath my arm. It was still a good kilometre to the village. The wind shrieked louder, driving its way in from the vast horizon. With every gust it became more unforgiving.

It was gone ten when we finally reached my parents' house, guided in by the lonely light in the window and the smoke that curled from the chimney. The gate leading into the front yard had slipped off one of its hinges. It scraped against the stone step as I opened it. My mother was already standing on the threshold in her housecoat. I immediately took off my gloves and rushed into her arms.

In the parlour, I stretched my fingers out towards the fire; my skin was so cold I couldn't yet bear to get too close.

"This is Anja," I said, remembering she was there. "I told you about her in my letter."

"You're very welcome," said my mother, but her expression grew quite stony. I tried to make sense of it for a second, but she turned her face from me.

"Anja, this is my grandmother, Rosetta, and my father, Ernst." I spoke to fill the silence as much as anything.

My grandmother was sitting in a rocking chair right beside the fire. She was still wearing her outdoor coat, although it was open, and a jumper underneath, and was tucked in to a crochet blanket. She was thinner than the last time I saw her, and the change in her was marked; she had always been so lively and animated.

I bent down to kiss her. "You look comfortable there," I said. Perhaps she shouldn't go home this time. There was plenty of room for her after all.

Anja extended her hand out to my father and seeming not to know quite what to do, he shook it. I observed the largeness of her hands and the firmness of her grip. He seemed to take notice of her suddenly.

"Lisbeth, the girls are perished," he said.

"There's stew on the fire," said my mother gesturing towards the kitchen, "and dumplings. There isn't much meat in it, I'm afraid, but we're all used to that these days, aren't we? Meat never did agree too well with my digestive system anyway. But there's plenty of bread, and as long as there's enough bread, nobody will go hungry in this house."

We sat at the table and I took the scarf from my head.

"Selina! What on earth have you done to your hair?"

Anja laughed. "I told you! Your face is too rectangular. Didn't I tell you, Selina?"

My hair was cut in the new bobbed style which finished at my jaw and curled round just beneath my earlobe. Everybody was doing it in Vienna.

"I didn't know for a second if you were a boy or a girl!" my grandmother piped up. Then she started coughing and in the end spat some phlegm into her handkerchief. I glanced at Anja's shorn hair and shifted uncomfortably in my seat.

"How are people taking the end of the war in Vienna?" asked my father. The wind howled so wildly inside the chimney breast I thought the fire would be extinguished.

"That depends on which people you mean," Anja told him. My father looked up, still clutching his fork with the dumpling skewered upon it. "The rich still maintain their places in the inner city, but their estates in Hungary, Czechoslovakia and Poland are all gone. Their wealth has been diminished, I think. Support grows daily for the Conservatives; the Democrats can't reasonably expect any kind of loyalty from the rich."

"A politician!" My father laughed to himself.

Anja's expression was dour. "Indeed. You look surprised, Herr Brunner."

He chuckled to himself. "Call me Ernst, please." My grandmother raised an eyebrow. "Only pleasantly," he said. "Tell me this, then: who would you rather have running the country, the Conservatives or the Democrats?"

"Neither, since the leader of the latter is a Jew. They are the enemy from within."

"Ha!" cried my father taking off his rabbit skin cap and placing it on the table next to his plate. "There's a fine line between a Democrat and a Bolshevik; you only have to ask the Russians!"

"Political discussions don't have any place at the dinner table, Ernst," my mother whispered, "and my mother hasn't got a clue what you're talking about."

But my father seemed to be enamoured of my friend with all her robust opinions.

"Well, I don't want either of them on the rampage," continued my father. "Jews or Bolsheviks."

"Let's hope the rest of the rural population feel the same," said Anja, "or there will be revolution within the year. The only way for us to survive now is to be unified with Germany."

With that all of my father's bluster seemed to die away and the laburnum tree whose branches had been flailing in the storm outside the window became still. "The French and the British would never allow it – nor the Americans." He picked up a chunk of bread and dipped it into his stew.

"Anyway," said my mother with affected gaiety, "enough of the French and the British. Let's leave politics to the politicians. Where were you thinking of staying tonight,

Anja?"

I felt my cheeks redden; Anja looked at me for help, as if she didn't quite know what she should say.

"She'll be fine in with me, Mother." I insisted. "There's plenty of room."

"No, there isn't!" My mother's voice was firm. "You'll be much more comfortable with Leon and Giselle," she said, turning to Anja. "They won't mind. Giselle always has the guest room made up these days, and Selina will tell you how restless I get with strangers in the house."

"No!" I heard myself shriek. It was as if my voice was coming from somewhere else. "His brothers are there. You can't, Anja!"

But my mother would hear none of it. "Selina, walk down the lane with Anja. Make sure you come straight back."

We walked through my parents' garden with the yellow light from the farm house fading behind us, past the rose bushes and holly. Nothing flowered this late in the year and the whole place was a tangle of thorns. The little gate which led out onto the track hadn't survived the evening's winds and was broken completely in two, with only a stump of it left swinging from its post.

"Anja," I began. I held up the gas lamp and her face was lit by its flickering glow. I could hear a fox howling way off in the distance. "I don't want you to go to Leon's."

She laughed, but I was deadly serious. I thought perhaps I could stow her away in one of the out buildings and bring her into the house once everyone was in bed, but my grandmother always slept downstairs when she stayed with us, propped up on pillows due to the difficulty of her breathing.

"Oh, Selina! Why ever not?" My mind started racing. If Anja were to be found in my room, our secret would surely be discovered. She groped in the darkness for my hand. "Really, Selina, I know the two of you used to have a thing together, but it's of no consequence now, is it? He's married, and your tastes…your tastes have changed."

"It isn't that!" I snapped. I braced myself to say it. I had only spoken of it once, and it all seemed so long ago now. I could almost feel their hands on me as I turned around – feel them pulling me to the floor, Elias's knee against my chest as I lay there helpless and trapped.

I looked wildly at Anja. "His brothers…" I stammered. "His brothers did something to me when I was young. It was the reason I moved to Vienna in the first place. It's the reason I am…as I am." I shocked myself as I said it. I put my hand to my mouth, as if to stuff the words back in. A lamb was squealing in the meadow, a horrible painful shriek. I looked into Anja's eyes. There was a terrible look, which I was unable to read. A gunshot went up from the fields, echoing through the night air. From a nearby farmhouse a young man came running out screaming, wearing only a pair of long johns. His chest was bare and his wiry frame bore the scars of shrapnel. It was pitiful to hear him, to see the sheer terror which contorted his gaunt face.

"Karl!" called a man's voice from the doorway. "It was just a shotgun, a farmer. It's alright, Karl." But the ghost-like figure kept on running. I could hear crying and a woman's voice whimper, "What have they done to my boy?"

"Anja!" I turned back to look at her, but that same impenetrable expression was locked onto her face like a mask.

"I'll hear no more of it!" she shouted, and stormed away from me further along the lane.

That night I could get no rest. I lay awake in my bed, watching the shadows stretching in through my window and the silhouettes of bats passing over the moon. I could hear my father snoring in the next room and the ticking of the clock in the hallway. In the end, I crept downstairs and took two drops of my mother's laudanum which she kept hidden away with the rest of the remedies she used for her ailments

– smelling salts, kaolin and peppermint oil – and staggered back upstairs in a daze. It wasn't long before my thoughts became misty and I was lost in sleep. I was back in Klimt's painting again, but this time it was I who was naked with Janika standing behind me. There were flowers floating on the air and mythical birds in cages, but as I turned my head to kiss her, I saw it wasn't Janika at all who was holding me, instead it was Luca with his hands that seemed too small for his body and his arms that were covered in wiry hairs. As I struggled and kicked against him he started pinching my breasts and shoving his hand roughly between my legs. I woke up screaming with my mother shouting my name, standing beside my bed holding a candle.

"Oh, Selina!" she cried. "Whatever's the matter?"

"A bad dream, that's all, Mother. Go back to bed."

"Have you taken something?" she demanded.

"No. Just herbal tea. I got it from a doctor in Vienna."

"What doctor?" She knew exactly what I'd done; the disappointment was written all over her face, the same as the night all those years ago when I came home late from Leon's house. She'd been so displeased with my flouting her rules that night, for coming home half an hour later than I should have done, that she hadn't even noticed my missing buttons or torn stockings. She turned away, tutted and slammed the door behind her.

It was mid-morning by the time Anja returned. I was out collecting the eggs from the coop ready for lunch. "How was it at Leon's?" I asked.

"Giselle was very hospitable," she replied curtly, "and so were Leon's brothers. Really, Selina, I know all about what you're doing. Do you think I don't read?" I didn't know what she was talking about. "There's a doctor in Vienna, a very well-renowned doctor who treats women for hysteria. In the beginning, scores of his patients were confiding that they'd been molested as children, but he couldn't bring a single case to a real conclusion, and really how likely are such widespread perversions against children? Most of them were accusing their own fathers! Selina, my own sister accused my father. It was a fantasy! Infantile fantasies and impulses are not the truth! They can ruin men's lives." I'd never seen her look so angry. "In the end, even the doctor himself abandoned his theories. Even he could see that the women were suffering from some kind of mental disorder. You need help, Selina. It's all lies!"

She didn't believe me! I'd confided in her that most secret of traumas and she didn't believe me! I was cornered by the confrontation – confused, as if I was beginning to doubt the truth of it myself. The memory of it had become obscure, caught up as it was in a web of nightmares and silence.

"Janika believed me!" I blurted out.

"Oh, your precious Janika!" she yelled.

"Yes, she did. And that's why I loved her so much more than I could ever love you!"

At that she slapped me so hard I almost wet myself, and not knowing what to do I dropped the eggs and they smashed on the yard in a sticky mess. I ran into the house and up to my brother's old room with my hand to my cheek so as to hide my shame. There on a tallboy beside his wash stand was a shaving bowl with a block of soap and a razor. I took the blade and felt the coolness of it against my skin. I felt the blood running against my wrist, the relief of it as it drained away from my body, purging me of all those vile feelings which surged through my veins, the poison which coursed through me. I saw my blood, crimson against his whitewashed floor. Outside, the clouds themselves seemed to turn to red. The wind chime, which hung from the eaves outside his room, clinked most discordantly, and the squawking from the chicken coop became distant and quiet. I saw Janika's face. We were back in the painting again; she was naked and she looked so peaceful with her head resting on my shoulder. But as she turned to look at me I saw she had no eyes. From the empty sockets she was crying and her tears were tears of blood. I reached for the curtains to steady myself. Everything went black.

The next thing I knew I was waking up in my bed. It was morning, the window was open enough to let in the fresh air, and I could hear the pigs squealing and the thudding of a hammer in the yard. The flowers were gone from my room and in their place was a bowl with a thermometer, a roll of bandages and a vial of laudanum beside it. My mother was dozing in the chair beside my bed. I reached across and stroked the back of her hand. She stirred and looked around the room, her eyes finally settling on my bound wrists.

"You missed the party," she said. "They arranged it in the village – to celebrate the end of the war and the safe return of the men. Everyone was there. I told them you were sick. They were all worried about you, especially Leon and Giselle," she paused for a moment, "…and Elias." I started to panic, had Anja said something to her? Betrayed that most intimate of secrets? "And your grandmother's devastated, Selina. How bloody selfish!"

She sat there with her back stiff and her face turned away from me. I propped myself up on my pillows. I could see Anja and my father working on the broken gate, they'd mended the splintered frame and cemented the post back into the ground. Anja looked just like a boy, dressed as she was in dungarees with all manner of tools sticking out of her front pocket.

"Let's just hope another storm doesn't come now to wreck it." He laughed. "Or the British, or the French."

"The Jews are Austria's real enemy," she was saying to him. "Their amorality and enervation sucks at the marrow of the Austrian people."

"Well," said my father, "it's refreshing to have someone in my household who sees eye to eye with me on politics, and one who can find her way around a tool box!" He slapped her on the back as if she was a man. "Very refreshing indeed."

"Don't bring that girl with you next time, Selina," said my mother, still gazing blankly out of the window. I'd thought I might stay; stay here in Tyrol and never go back to Vienna, but my mother's meaning was quite clear. *Don't bring her next time* – next time I visited. There was little that got past my mother. She knew. She knew then and there what I was. If only she'd been so sharp-eyed that night all those years ago. I supposed there were things she could suffer to look at and things so ugly even she would have to turn her head away. She picked up the bowl and the dressings from the table.

"She's not welcome in my house," she reiterated, and left me alone closing the door behind her.

Chapter Ten

"That will be fifteen Kronen, Fräulein Brunner," Herr Levine told me, holding my necklace in the palm of his hand. The pawnbroker's was uncommonly busy. Most of the customers were women in overcoats. Everybody had something to sell; nobody was buying.

Fifteen? "Surely that can't be right? That's more than double the amount you paid for it!"

"I know," said Herr Levine, "but it is the state of the nation, unfortunately. This depression won't last much longer, then you will be able to buy yourself a dozen pearls!"

I doubted that. I looked at the jewellery cabinet, it was heaving with gem stones and bits of gold, full of things nobody could afford to buy back.

The woman behind me in the queue started sighing and shuffling her feet.

"Very well," I said reaching for my purse.

I considered the fifteen Kronen an extortionate sum of money then for the return of my necklace. Little did I know that two years later I'd pay a hundred and eighty for it, and the year after that, eighty three thousand. Money meant nothing any more. I saw people pushing it in wheelbarrows down Ringstrasse, too much of it for anyone to ever count. It had to be taken on trust, and a week later the sum of it was virtually worthless anyway.

But the years following the end of the war brought with them a generous wind. Under the coalition headed by the Social Democrats, Karl-Marx-Hof was born. The council set about building laundry facilities, a library, community college, a hospital and public baths. At first, people complained; there were heaps of rubble lying everywhere and men perched on girders eating their sandwiches thirty feet above the street. But as the building projects were nearing completion there seemed to be a feeling of euphoria almost, which rang about the province. The new amenities were utilitarian, lacking the architectural grandeur of Ringstrasse, but at least we'd got them, and all without any threat of revolution whatsoever.

Anja and I walked home arm in arm after work. The sun was still up and I could hear men whooping and hollering on the other side of the railway embankment. They emerged from over the brow of the hill, running breathlessly, a pack of them, led by Rudi Martin who'd taken his shirt off and was swinging it like a lasso above his head. We knew what all the excitement was about – it was the same for us in the factory: the working day had been reduced to eight hours and there were two weeks a year paid holiday for all of us.

"How will you two spend all that extra time?" he asked, falling into step with Anja and putting his arm roughly around her shoulder.

"Get off me!" she cried, giving him a playful poke in the belly. "You're covered in sweat." His body was wet with it, and smeared with coal dust from the railway which glistened upon his midriff in a sparkling black sheen.

"What will you do, Rudi?" I asked him.

He shrugged. "Get drunk, pick fights, jump on a few girls." He looked remarkably pleased with himself as he elbowed Anja in the ribs.

As for me, I'd never known such idleness. We didn't even get out of bed for two days, Anja and I. We just lay there in our vests and stockings, eating great wedges of a custard tart, smoking cigarettes, making love. We talked all day about nothing in particular. I told her how my grandmother used to keep a dressing up box and I spent half my childhood wearing her long strings of beads and lace collars with my cheeks covered in rouge. "I must have always wanted to go before the camera," I told her.

She just shrugged and said make-up and jewellery never interested her. "Wouldn't it be good to be a man?" she asked. "Just for a day. Would you if you could?"

"I suppose so, just to see what it was like, but not Herr Auer!" I said. "Nor Herr Lehner! Perhaps I'd be Rudi Martin, though, just to see."

Anja laughed. "Let's go to Ringstrasse!" she said. "Let's walk down the road hand in hand, kiss each other outside the opera house and just see what everybody does." We didn't, though, but we did go to an exhibition in town and went window shopping and for coffee with some of the other girls.

The time went way too quickly though and soon we were back at Schwestern Flöge.

It was the first day back when one of the other seamstresses collapsed at her toil. A few of the other women went rushing from their stations and fussed about her, loosening her buttons and fanning her with bits of cloth. But as soon as she was restored she doubled over and put her hands to her belly. I took my foot off the treadle and went running to Fräulein Flöge's office. Madam Poiret was with her, drinking tea. She was quite grey now and heavier. The handle of her porcelain cup looked tiny beside her swollen fingers.

"Pardon the intrusion, Fräulein Flöge," I said breathlessly, "but one of the women from the production room's collapsed – I think her baby's coming early."

Fräulein Flöge often said she despaired of the number of pregnancies on her shop floor. It was an epidemic, she said. The husbands would do well to control themselves a little better; perhaps then there wouldn't be the incessant whining for more wages. The German Workers' Party never seemed to tire of it.

"Is there anyone who could perhaps take her to the community hospital in Karl-Marx-Hof?" I asked.

"Yes, of course, Selina." Fräulein Flöge immediately uncrossed her legs and rose to her feet. "I shall send my driver straight away."

79

At that, Madame Poiret snorted. "Community hospital? *Red Vienna!* That's what this place has become. How much more money are the Democrats planning on pouring into that communist ghetto? People say Karl-Marx-Hof has turned into some kind of proletarian holiday resort! How do they pay for it all? Soaking the middle classes, that's how! Do you know there are ladies I keep company with having to wear gold plate these days!" She tutted and replaced the cup in her saucer.

Nobody ever had enough money, especially those of us working in the factories or on the railroads but we'd expected that almost, with the end of the war.

There were anti-coalition mutterings to be heard along Ringstrasse, but only from rich ladies in the queue for the opera house or sat outside pavement cafés drinking coffee. Nobody had anything better to talk about; none of them looked even remotely like activists. In the end they got what they wanted by lawful means.

In November 1920, the majority vote was won by the Christian Social Party, and where would that leave the workers? We were back to square one.

Chapter Eleven
1931

The years rolled by for Anja and me with little event. Nothing changed – not for the likes of us, anyway. Perhaps I'd expected too much. A life of tedium and hard work, of collapsing exhausted into bed always seemed good enough for my mother. I could almost hear her voice the minute the thought entered my head. It seemed impossible so much time could have passed since I first made my way here from Tyrol.

Anja was standing in the kitchen cooking up some fish heads in a pan. "More Jews coming in from Germany," she commented, leafing through a newspaper which lay on the counter at her side. She'd grown shapeless, I thought, and thick around the waist. "As if there aren't enough people out of work as it is." She was right about that at least. It had been a terrible winter; beggars huddled freezing in the alley behind our rooms while the snow eddied dizzily on the swirling winds. It felt as if I was earning less money now than during the war.

I shrugged. "I heard they were mostly artists and film-makers. The Nazis won't let them work in Germany anymore." What had people like that got to do with the likes of us?

"There are artisans, too," she said coldly, spooning the bisque into bowls, "and unskilled labourers. I don't like it, Selina, that's all."

After lunch, we made our way down to the allotments. It was late March; I wasn't convinced all threat of frost had passed but Anja was right. If we didn't start planting now, our stores would soon run dry.

We'd rented a plot just off the Danube canal, an offshoot of the river just north of the downtown area with pathways lining its banks. It made for a pleasant stroll some days. The old fishermen always liked to pass the time of day with a woman and there were Roma living on barges with copper kettles hanging in the windows, which they'd decorated by hand with all kinds of beautiful floral motifs. The allotments themselves lay back from the pathway behind a wooden fence. We'd become somewhat of a community down there, sharing tea and gardening utensils, and discussing which crops to plant. For our own part, we sowed onions, red cabbage, potatoes, beans and pumpkins, and we had rows of raspberry and gooseberry canes lined up along the partition fence. Anja had insisted on a few sunflowers as well. They were her favourites; they brightened her, she said.

I admit I quite enjoyed the feel of the earth between my fingers; it reminded me of my parents' farm back in Tyrol. I looked over at Anja who was picking slugs off the ground. There we both were, wearing rolled up dungarees and head scarfs. She got up, rubbing the arch of her back, turned to me and smiled. I leaned against my fork, looking almost through her towards one of the furthest plots which was thick with foxgloves and stinging nettles and strewn with bits of masonry.

There was a woman surveying the tangle of greenery which overran her little patch of land. It was Neomi. She was older now. I supposed we all were, but she was as slender as ever and looked elegant still in a floral blouse which was knotted up just above her belly and a pair of maroon pants. I dropped my fork on the ground and made my way over to her. Her hair was kinked. It looked nice; she must have taken to curling it.

"You'll need more than that, Neomi," I said, seeing the trowel in her hand.

Her expression was one of weakness. "I've paid the first month's rent in advance."

At that I hooted. "Oh Neomi! Without coming to see it first?" I felt almost sorry for her, though I don't suppose she deserved it in the least, only she looked so lovely standing there. I started pulling at the weeds. "Some of this is mint," I said. "I can smell it, leave it in. It's good for tea, especially for morning sickness or indigestion. You could trade it; everyone's pregnant these days." She stared at the plot as if she didn't know where she should start. "Have you not got any gloves?"

I shielded my eyes and looked back over to Anja who was glowering at me through the window of the allotment sheds.

"Livia's gone," she blurted out. That was about right; that one only ever did care about herself. "To Berlin. She was only meant to be going for three weeks – it was some low budget film, but that was in October... She isn't coming back."

It was difficult not to feel sympathy for her. We were both the same. "And what of you, Neomi?" I asked.

She looked as if she might cry. "Still a bit of modelling work sometimes. Mainly catalogues, though, now, and I work in a little cosmetics shop off Ringstrasse on Saturdays. The extra money's allowed me to come back here at least. My old place was horrible... Anyway, what should I plant? I've no idea really."

I looked at the plot for a while. "Something that other people haven't got. Maybe some trees; cherry, apple and pear – one of each." They wouldn't yield any fruit this year, I conceded, but next year it would all be worth the wait. "And kale... Oh and some root vegetables: beetroot and turnips, some carrots, and you could keep the mint and stick some other herbs in, especially chives; they grow like weeds." I thought for a moment. "Chickens!" I said, thinking of my parents' yard. "Get some chickens and you'll always have eggs. I'll help you, Neomi. It will be good."

I'd not found any joy in anything in a long time. *Way too long.*

Neomi and I worked on like that all afternoon until we'd cleared the area to a barren patch of soil with channels running along it where the seedlings would go. My palms were blistered where they'd rubbed against the handle of my shovel; I'd not even noticed the pain while I was working.

The sun was setting and the clouds glowed pink, sitting low on the horizon. I could hear the sound of a violin coming from one of the barges – not the constrained music of the opera house, something jubilant, the unbound song of a fiddler, mingling with laughter and the tapping of feet against the decks.

"Thank you," said Neomi extending her hand.

"You're welcome." I found myself smiling despite myself.

That night there was a pot of chicken soup left at my door. I ate it instead of Anja's fish heads. Anja slammed her pot of bisque down with a bang on the counter. Broth splattered all over the kitchen window and the walls.

I couldn't even bear the thought of sewing seams the following morning. Plasma seeped out through my bandages and it was all I could do to lift up my basket. But it was a good feeling, that my injuries had come from hard work, from helping a friend, rather than from old anger turned inwards. I may not have achieved great things in Vienna, but perhaps it was the small victories that mattered most of all.

"What on earth have you done?" asked Fräulein Flöge when she saw me on the factory floor.

"I was planting vegetables most of the weekend," I told her, "and I helped out an old friend of mine as well, clearing away a few weeds."

She raised an eyebrow. "You like gardening?"

"I've taken on an allotment." I lowered my voice and leaned forward, taking her into my confidence. "I share it with one of the girls in the cutting room... Times are hard; sometimes there isn't enough food."

Fräulein Flöge flushed scarlet. She turned on her heels and marched back towards her office.

After lunch, she called me in to see her. I prepared

myself for a telling off; I'd only completed one garment all morning. There were piles of paper everywhere and the place was quite dishevelled. Even the plants looked in desperate need of water. "Frau Huber is retiring at the end of the month," she said briskly, "and I shall need some help in the office, answering the phone, typing and so on. You can go to evening class if you aren't up to speed. There will be some extra money in it for you of course." I could have kissed her right then. "Very good," she snapped. "Back to the shop floor, please."

I asked Neomi to come for coffee with me, nowhere special, just a little café around the corner from our rooms, to celebrate my good news. The coffee was bad and the tablecloths were made from vinyl.

"It will be nice to get back into some decent clothes," I told Neomi. "Fräulein Flöge has let me have a skirt and two blouses. All I need now are a few pairs of stockings." My voice faltered. Her own legs were bare and streaky, as if she'd rubbed them with tea.

Neomi smiled. "It's been a long time coming. It's a shame you didn't make it as a model; you're still a very attractive woman."

She flattered me; I'd ruined myself with cigarettes and too much coffee. "It's a shame Janika never felt the same way!"

"Well, I know all about that!" Neomi laughed contemptuously. "Unrequited love they call it, don't they? In any relationship there's always one who loves more than the other. Next time I shall make sure I'm the one calling the shots."

She was right. I thought of Anja with her fish heads and her opinions. "Still no news of Livia?" I asked.

She shook her head and looked down into her coffee cup.

Anja was drunk by the time I got back to my room. She was just there, slumped on my bed in her brassiere and knickers with a bottle of absinthe in her hand.

"Where have you been?" she slurred.

"Just with Fräulein Flöge. She's offered me a job in the office; we were sorting out the finer details, that's all."

"You liar!" she shouted. "You bloody liar!" The bottle of absinthe shattered against the wall, scattering shards of glass all over my bed. "You've been with that filthy Jew!"

I resisted the impulse to slap her face; she would have been too drunk even to put up her hand to protect herself.

"Love them, don't you?" she was shrieking with tears in her eyes. "First Janika and now her! Well, let me tell you, Selina, something's coming. Something righteous and invincible and when it does, Austria will be purged of them all." Her voice quietened and became quite sinister. "Are you sure you're not one?" she whispered.

The look in her eyes made me afraid.

I threw her shirt and trousers at her. "Get dressed, Anja."

"No." She undid her brassiere and began running her fingers all over her breasts, then she slid her hands between her legs and lay stroking herself, at first gently and then more frantically. It looked ugly. She started to cry. "What's wrong, Selina? Isn't this what your precious Janika used to do?"

Chapter Twelve

"Fräulein Flöge takes two sugars," Frau Huber explained. "Brown, not white. Except when she has guests; then you will be expected to go to the patisserie and get some apple cake. When she has pastries she does not take sugar."

I nodded.

"Take the money out of petty cash." Frau Huber opened her drawer and showed me an enamel tin. "Write out a docket to show how much you have taken out and what for, cash up the tin every Friday and ask the cashier for extra float if needs be."

There was nothing Frau Huber didn't know about the running of the office; she'd been there eighteen years, after all. She went about clearing her few belongings from her desk: some faded photographs, a ballpoint pen and a faux leather travel clock. Not much really for nearly two decades' work. Schwestern Flöge had been run like a well-oiled machine since her arrival.

I tried to listen to all her instructions; I only hoped I could live up to her legacy.

As soon as I arrived back at Waldstrasse, I changed out of my skirt and blouse, and into my dungarees and jackboots. I hung my work attire on scented hangers which I kept in my cupboard for my best clothes; I'd thought only of Neomi all day.

When I arrived at the allotments, the mosquitos were already rallying low on the banks of the Danube and barges belonging to the Roma had gathered at the lock. I could smell a hog roasting somewhere; I'd not eaten meat since Neomi's chicken soup. Neomi herself didn't look well.

She'd carried some lengths of redwood and a roll of chicken wire all the way from the hardware store.

"I'm worn out before we even start, Selina!" She smiled at me faintly. I traced the line of her clavicle where her blouse fell open at the collar. She was skinnier even than the week before.

"It isn't a hard job," I told her. "I made one once with my brother back in Tyrol."

I must have looked sad because she took my hand and stroked it with her fingers. "It's a long time, I think, since you've been there?"

I nodded and listened to the evensong and the distant chugging of engines beside the lock. But the silence soon becoming awkward, I fetched some tools from the shed and a couple of oil lamps which I placed on the ground. The light would soon be dim. I stood with my hands on my hips; it would be laborious without my brother.

Just then, one of the narrow boats turned off its engine and a man shouted, "Ahoy there!" from the deck – one of the Roma from the Danube. He stopped whittling the stick he was working on and tipped his hat to us; his long hair hung around his face. "A lady carpenter! I never saw one of those before. You need a hand, Fräulein?"

"No! Thank you, no," I called back.

He laughed to himself and went back to his carving.

Neomi put her hand to her brow. "We can't pay you," she told him.

"A kiss then?" he suggested. "A kiss from both of you?"

She put down her roll of wire, stepped up onto the boat and kissed him on both cheeks.

He whistled to himself. "That's what I like – a friendly type of lady. It's a lonely life on the water."

I supposed it would have been. I'd heard Rudi before, bemoaning them. *River rats,* he called them, lighting fires, dumping rubbish everywhere they went, not to mention charming the women with all their mystery and exotic ways. For my own part, the idea of drifting, of having no particular purpose, no work to do, no Herr Auer on my back every week – that appealed to me more than I dared to admit.

Camlo, he told us his name was. "It means lovely," he said. "Names are very important, aren't they?" When I told him mine he thought for a moment and said, "Ah, goddess of the moon. See, it's true, you're a goddess and you've come to me in the light of the moon."

Even I couldn't help but laugh at that. There was a cheek about him, that was for certain.

"Let's have a look at this coop," he said, stepping off his boat onto the bank and walking towards Neomi's little plot of land. He picked up one of the planks and turned it over in his hand, then held it up to his nose. "I love the smell of redwood… Lenza!" he called to a man on one of the other boats. He tipped his hat again. "I don't mind doing this at all for you," he said, "but you could do something for me. My boat's in a disgusting state. Maybe we could help each other out, couldn't we, now that we're all friends?"

And that was how Neomi's chicken coop came to be built, by the two Roma from the Danube. She promised to call her first two chickens Camlo and Lenza.

Camlo wasn't joking about the state of his home. The two of us looked at each other in horror as we ducked inside the boat. The whole place stank of whisky and the sink was overflowing with cups and plates with dried food caked onto them. The windows were greasy, and God only knew what fell from his sheets when I shook them out. I spent most of the evening up to my elbows in laundry soap chipping away at the food and Neomi found a sweeper in a little utility cupboard opposite the stove. I initially thought the carpet to be a mottled green, but as she ran the sweeper back and forth, a floral pattern began to emerge from beneath the grime. I bundled up his sheets to take them home with me to wash and found some clean bedding in a drawer underneath his bed.

After all that was done, I cooked him some sausages on his stove and brought them out to him with a crust of bread. He'd constructed a kind of triangular frame and was stretching some wire around it. "I'll make the shelter and the perches tomorrow," he said. "There are plenty of branches along the banks. Perhaps later you'd like to come with me for a stroll while I look for them, Selina?"

"Yes, that would be nice."

On one of the other boats, somebody began to play the harmonica, its melody slow and haunting. I found myself wondering why there was no woman about the place. "Didn't you ever want to lay down some roots?" I asked him as he ate.

"I have, in my own way, I suppose. I like the Danube; I might stay for a while. Every waterway has its own character; in Venice the canal reeks and there's no shade, the Seine would swallow you up if you let it, and it's black as tar. I like the people here."

"In Vienna? I never heard anyone say that before."

"I like you," he said.

It was midnight by the time Neomi and I started making our way back to Waldstrasse. The moon was full and bright; foxes were rummaging around the empty oil drums and potato sacks. Clouds were creeping in front of the moon. There was a beautiful glowing light for a moment, in shades of indigo and violet, but suddenly it was as if a cloak had drawn itself around us and everything was plunged into blackness. She held my hand as we turned onto the track which led from the canal side all the way back to Waldstrasse.

"I could never have managed it without you," she said. "Thank you for helping with the allotment." She turned and kissed me softly on the lips.

I held her close, longing for the sensation of her naked body against mine, but she'd grown so bony of late, it was just like holding a boy. I caressed her hair, but she drew back.

"Selina," she said gently, "it wasn't meant to be that kind of kiss."

The darkness hid my blushes. "Would it be so bad?" I

thought of the way she used to shout and swear, up in her room with Livia, and me living my solitary life downstairs, aching with loneliness.

"We're both in love with other people," she said.

I shook my head. "I don't love Anja."

"I wasn't talking about her."

We walked on for a while with the silence weighing heavily upon us. There was no queue for the opera house that night, making Ringstrasse eerily quiet.

"More and more Austrians are boycotting the opera," whispered Neomi eventually. "The German officials don't come here anymore." She narrowed her eyes, seeming to ponder on the implications of it for a time. "I don't like it, Selina… I see things… All this will end very badly for us."

"It's just politics, Neomi." I shrugged. "I leave all that to Anja."

"Well, maybe you shouldn't."

We held each other's gaze. She was right; there was this indeterminable thing lurking in the shadows, swirling invisibly on the Viennese wind.

I followed Neomi up the front steps at the lodging house.

"Jonas!" She leant across the counter to kiss him on the cheek. He was an old man now, a sad figure, I thought, now that his capricious friends were no longer there. Where were they, all those handsome young men and women dressed in feathers? Their spirits were all still there somewhere, those glimmers from the past, just like Janika, just like Klimt. We could no longer feel them with us, that was all. He gave us our respective keys and Neomi stayed chatting to him while I went upstairs to my room.

"I'm sorry," I told Anja, throwing my keys down on the table. I couldn't help but feel pity for her, just as I'd done the night before when she lay there caressing herself, just wanting me to love her.

"Did you finish off the coop?" she asked.

"Nearly." I was glad at least there was no malice in her voice, no argument bubbling just under the surface.

We made love that night, but there was no satisfaction for either of us. In the end, I lay there staring into the void of my room while Anja drifted off to sleep.

The women in the factory didn't like my new position at Schwestern Flöge. At break time, nobody even gave me a light from their cigarette. They stopped talking when I walked out onto the floor, shuffling their feet and refusing to make eye contact.

Away from their glare, I was enjoying it. I took telephone calls from designers and wealthy clients, placed orders for bolts of silk. I took minutes in meetings and fetched pastries for the Flöge sisters' guests. The money made a welcome change as well. I was now the proud owner of a bottle of nail polish, a ceramic powder compact and a satin purse. I curled my hair and wore lipstick to the office.

Then one day a man arrived without an appointment; he opened the door and walked in without hesitation.

"Emilie!" he said as Fräulein Flöge stood up from her desk. He pressed her hand and looked at her with solemnity in his eyes. I thought she must know him because she didn't struggle in the least. He was a tall man, as broad as any farm hand from Tyrol, although wearing an expensive suit and a gold pin.

"The *Creditanstalt* is in trouble. You must go and empty your account immediately."

Fräulein Flöge put her hand to her face. "Oh, Harvey!" she whispered with the colour draining from her cheeks. She pulled back the little canvas on the wall, which Klimt had painted for her and frantically turned the dials to the safe. She took out a pile of papers and sifted through them on her desk.

She barely looked in my direction. "Get out, Selina!"

The following day the news came that the bank had collapsed. People blamed the Rothschilds – Jews – and the Conservatives for ever trusting them in the first place. I was glad I'd kept my few spare Schillings in a jar.

Chapter Thirteen

On Thursdays, I went to the municipal college so that I might be instructed in shorthand and typing and all matters secretarial. I was nearing the end of my two-year course; it had been a hard road, shall we say. I was the oldest in my class, joining at the age of thirty-three. The other girls were all only twenty-one at most but seemed far more proficient than me. We sat in the stark little room week after week going over endless exercises: *'asdf ölkj ... asdf ölkj'* to the clacking rhythm whose tempo quickened with the passing of autumn then winter then spring. Now it was nearly Christmas and there was an air of excitement at the thought of the impending certificates and grading of our work. Even I, who in the beginning was slow and cack-handed, could now reach speeds of forty words a minute on a good day. When we left that evening, there was an assembly of women outside, protesting about the lack of educational opportunities available for the female sex.

"It's Engelbert Dollfuss," Anja informed me later, "and that Christian Social Party. *Social* they call themselves. The whole thing smacks of fascism if you ask me."

I wasn't interested. We went off to the December Market that night; it came to town every winter from Frankfurt and stayed open until ten. Temporary stalls had been erected in the piazza, to look like alpine wood cabins. It was a place full of pleasure, where traders laid out wooden toys and fancy soaps, knitted pom-pom hats and handmade candles. The cold was biting but there was bratwurst on sale and hot mulled wine, and huge pans of garlic mushrooms which they served in cardboard containers with fries. There were beer stalls and coffee tents, jugglers and musicians.

Some of the Roma also ran stalls. I was surprised, pleasantly so, to see Camlo there on a stall filled with little wooden animals which he'd carved himself. All sorts: frogs, hogs, all various sizes, all with a line of ridges along their back and a carved baton in their mouths. When you ran the baton over the ridges, the animal made a sound: a grunt or a croak. Quite a crowd had gathered; his carvings were very lifelike.

"Selina!" he called when he saw me. His hair was tied back and hung in a ponytail from under his trilby. "For you." He handed me down a wooden heart painted with white flowers with a loop of flax for hanging.

"I couldn't possibly," I told him. It was a beautiful thing, though.

"A gift," he said, taking off his hat and giving a small bow.

I broke into a smile and a woman from the crowd let out a little *'Ahh'* sound.

Anja pulled me away but I found I kept looking back over my shoulder. In the end, she marched back to the stall and handed him a fistful of Schillings.

I didn't buy much, only some stollen and a bag full of mulling spices: cinnamon sticks, dried oranges and cloves. I thought I might use them with some sugar and apple juice, or even some wine. I could invite Neomi over. I bought a muslin bag full of dried lavender for Anja's Christmas present; I thought she could hang it up in her wardrobe so as to keep her clothes smelling nice, and a vial of bath oil which was scented with sandalwood.

The following evening was far less festive. Anja persuaded me in the end to go to Rudi's meeting. It was held in a darkened room behind the cobblers'. The curtains were drawn in and, although the candles burned quite low, I could see enough to gauge that the whole room was covered in grime. I imagined black beetles crawling in the filth underneath the table and mice raiding the grain store beyond the back door. We were crammed in from the doorway all the way over to the stove. Some were seated around a large table in the centre of the room but the majority were standing, their hot bodies crushed up against one another.

Most of those present seemed to be from the railway – men in woollen jackets and flat caps with weathered faces and expressions of angst. There was some kind of debate going on about the provident fund that had been set up; the workers should think about bigger contributions, Rudi was saying, if any form of strike were to succeed.

"And that's where the company's got us over a barrel," one of the older men said. He sat cradling a little dog in the crook of his elbow. "As if the wages are high enough to put any aside for any kind of fund! I haven't a Schilling in my pocket."

There were scant murmurs of assent from one or two of the others, but most were shouting insults. "You washed up old coward!" I heard one of them say. "Our children are on their knees from want of a warm coat and a hot meal!"

"I was only thinking the price of a loaf of bread, that's all," Rudi explained. "Without the fund there's nothing to save us from starvation."

The old man swirled his beer around in his tankard and finally took a glug before slamming it down against the table. The dog scampered away through the back door. I could smell the bland aroma of potatoes and cabbage wafting in from one of the other tenements.

"And once we've saved enough for forty days' bread, the company will be quaking in their boots at the size of our *fund*?" asked the old man. "We'll come out of it defeated and worse off! A month from now we'll be begging them to take us back on for two thirds of what they're paying us now!" Outside, the painful whine of a fox could be heard. The little dog came dashing back in and leapt onto his master's lap for protection. "See!" said the man.

I cleared my throat. "Surely it's better to come to some kind of understanding?" I suggested. "In any strike the workers always suffer far worse than the companies themselves."

"What are you doing here anyway, Selina Brunner?" one of the women demanded. "You'll be taking your little list into Fräulein Flöge, I bet, first thing in the morning, telling her who was in here, planning dissent behind her back."

"I promise you I shan't!" I protested. "Times are as hard for me as they are for anyone else."

"Pah!" said the woman, and one of the others gave me a dig in the back.

"I've heard enough of this!" cried the old man. "Ruin one side and kill the other if it amuses you. Build up your stash of Schillings and see how far it gets you! I'll hear no more of this!" He rose to his feet and made his way through the throng of people with his dog trailing at his heels.

When Christmas itself came, I cooked mutton stew. I'd invited Neomi over but she declined. It hurt me a little bit more every year that I wasn't in Tyrol with my family. I could have gone there, I supposed, but the shame of what I'd put them through prevented me. It was an accident. I'd never meant to take my own life; there was just something inside of me that I needed to let out. Then there was the other thing: the feeling somehow that I was a stranger to them, that I was in some way locked outside their world, looking in on them through a pane of glass. There was no animosity between us – on the contrary, in fact. My mother wrote to me and sent Christmas cards over the years.

'I hope we haven't offended you in any way. You're welcome here at any time. Your nieces and nephews have been asking to meet you.'

I missed her, sometimes so much it hurt. But here I was, in my room with Anja, whom I didn't love in the slightest, sitting over a dinner which was mostly made out of pearl barley and potatoes from the allotment. There were a few paper lanterns we'd made, dotted about the place, and some cards from the other boarders, but there was no gaiety, no children, no family here; only Anja who pushed her food around her plate with her fork. She tried her best to be pleasant, but I supposed she must have felt disappointed. She'd made me a set of ivory pyjamas, with small pearl buttons and a plain collar. She must have been saving up for the fabric all year, thought about the gift week by week, stacking up her pile of Schillings.

"Try them on," she urged. She must have known I hadn't wanted to. I made love to her that night only out of a sense of duty. I felt I should do, that was all.

I rose early on Boxing Day. Anja still lay sleeping with her mouth open and the stew sat congealed in its dish upon the table. I took her coat, which was thicker and warmer than mine, and wrapped my scarf around my head. All was quiet as I walked through the allotments back towards the Danube. Snow lay glittering in the frail sunlight and the trees and the fruitless blackberry bushes were crusted with frost. I squeezed myself between the broken fence panels onto the tow path, but the canal was abandoned. There was no smoke, no flames dancing in the empty oil drums. The narrowboats and the strings of washing slung between them. All were gone. The only thing left was the water, which was muddy and thick with ice. I turned away from it. I hadn't realised until then how much I longed to see him. The loneliness, that had been gone from me of late but never far away, began swirling around me like a freezing wind. I was looking for something sharp on the ground, a piece of broken glass maybe, or a piece of barbed wire, but everything was covered in snow. In panic, my eyes flitted all over the banks. Then I remembered the blood, and the feeling of life drifting from me. I saw the disappointment on my mother's face as she sat at my bedside. I took a deep breath and composed myself, lowering my head; even the points on the hawthorn bushes held some allure for me as I made my way back to Waldstrasse. But I didn't go to them, and later of course I was glad of that. It shocked me though, that this part of me – this demon I had thought long gone –

was still there, raging against the fragile restraints that held it. I was never so afraid of it as I was then.

The next morning, I tried to rouse Anja for work but she just muttered and shooed me away. She rolled over and showed me her back. In the end, I took her coat again, but my hands were uncovered as I went out into the street. Karl-Marx-Hof was eerily quiet as I walked through the streets towards the factory. Most of the windows still had the blankets nailed across them; they hadn't yet been pulled back so that the pale sunlight might stir the inhabitants within. It was a harsh wind that whistled along the Strasse, so unforgiving it made my eyes stream, and the hot tears froze quickly against my cheek. There wasn't even a drop of warmth emanating from the baker's shop or the launderette as I passed them, nor the hot smoke from the foundry. As I made my way over the bridge the railway below was silent. Its tracks ebbed away into the mouth of a tunnel, strewn with pitchforks and shovels. This was it. Strike.

Schwestern Flöge was open for business. The gates had been pulled back and there was a gaggle of women in the courtyard, warming their hands around a fire which was burning quite low in a steel drum. Some of them sheltered their children underneath their skirts for warmth. Some held home-made placards, daubed with slogans:

A fair day's work for a fair day's pay! and *Justice for the workers!*

As I passed them, one of the women reached out and touched my sleeve.

"Will you join us, Selina?"

"This isn't the way." I said.

I went into the factory, hung up my coat in the cloakroom and seated myself at one of the machines. There were pieces of a dress in a basket beside the treadle which had been pinned together ready for stitching. I wound up the bobbin and threaded up the machine.

"Selina!" Fräulein Flöge appeared in the production room. "What are you doing?"

"I thought I might be of more use in here."

"Oh, no! That won't do. You must come with me at once."

I replaced the cloth cover on the machine and went with Fräulein Flöge. There were hardly any women in the production room, or at the cutting tables either, but as I followed her down the corridor I could feel their eyes burning into me.

"What do they want?" she asked once we were safely away in her office.

My eyes flitted around the room. The porcelain tea service still sat on its silver tray, the Dutch Old Masters were still held fast to the wall, and through the window I could see the Flöges' driver sitting idly in their motorcar.

"The women are having to sell what little they have for food and fuel," I told her. "And when that goes, what next? They need higher wages or they'll starve."

Fräulein Flöge started wringing her hands. "But by the day, money is worth less and less. It melts away whilst I am sleeping. I did not cause this catastrophe; the ruin is spreading through Europe like wildfire. Tell me what I should do!"

I shook my head. "I don't know."

"If I paid them in food?" she suggested.

"And have them reduced to bartering? Is that what Vienna's become? They want the means to pay for their own food!"

She turned her back and I returned to the production room, seating myself with the few other seamstresses who turned up for work that day. The next thing I knew, she too sat down at one of the machines. I nodded to her as she plucked one of the pinned garments from her basket and lifted up the foot of her machine.

On the way home, the streets were more alive, although there was not the noisy clatter of the tram, and the cafeterias and the bakeries were still shut up. As I approached the railway, the pickets were shouting and hurling rocks onto the track. I looked over the bridge. There were Roma gone to work in place of the railway men. How they'd made their way in through the curls of barbed wire was a mystery to me, but they were being protected by soldiers who now fired a round of artillery over the heads of the strikers. The noise of it was so loud I could feel it pounding inside my body. I pulled my hood over my head and ran towards Karl-Marx-Hof, not daring to look back but sensing somehow that the crowd was dispersing behind me.

The strike went on for longer than anyone could have imagined. The men went to bed sober in Karl-Marx-Hof. No one possessed even a lump of coal to put upon their fires. The baker and the grocer for a while extended their credit but within days even they were forced to shut their doors. Dogs and cats were turned out onto the streets and went scavenging through the almost empty dustbins. Even the ladies of the night in the alley behind Waldstrasse knocked down their prices. Only the bailiff and the pawnbrokers rejoiced. Every stick of furniture went to them bit by bit and the workers would surely be in too much debt once the strike was over to ever buy it back. At dusk, not a single light went on and Anja complained that she didn't know whether to light her candle or to eat it.

"You could always go back to work," I suggested.

She avoided even dignifying that with a reply.

I think it was the factory women who broke first. It hadn't been thought through properly and they'd begun the strike before the provident fund could swell sufficiently to keep them. But the men still refused to go back. It is incredible how dogged the human spirit can be once it resolves to dig in. Their funds were empty. In the end, it was sheer determination that kept them going.

Then, just as everyone was on the verge of giving up anyway, the government sent the army against them and arrested some of the strikers. A political solution could not be found. Urged on by Mussolini, Dollfuss declared parliamentary government unworkable and suspended parliament indefinitely. He began governing on the basis of a War Emergency Powers decree dating from the war. All other political factions were banned. Fascists, Nazis and Communists, he said, were enemies of what should be a Christian, ethnically German state.

This only served to energise the people's army – the Schutzbund.

For two days it was chaos. The Schutzbund barricaded themselves into our housing estate and soon police and paramilitaries took up positions outside the stronghold.

"We'll have to leave," said Anja, throwing a few of our clothes into a carpet bag. "I heard the college is giving refuge to women and children."

I looked quickly around my room. I knew the police wouldn't tolerate the stand-off for long.

"Alright," I said. It was a long time since I'd felt so scared. I snatched up my necklace and a photograph of Janika. I couldn't recall thinking of her these last months, so I don't know why I should have at that moment.

Neomi, I thought, but it was silly. She'd already be at the synagogue; I doubted there was any way back for her to Karl-Marx-Hof until the fighting was over. The elevator wasn't working and the ground floor of our boarding house was crammed with railwaymen and unskilled labourers. Some lined the stairs to the first floor and others were crouching by the front windows. The Schutzbund had kicked out the glass and sat poised with their guns.

Too many men.

I quailed as I weaved my way through them. One of them laughed as I passed him. I tried to keep my knees together as I descended the stairs. There was no sign of Jonas anywhere. Part of me didn't want to leave the building, to be at the mercy of police and paramilitaries. Finally, the doors were thrown open, the men flattened themselves underneath the windows and Anja and I were thrown out into the street. Outside, the police lowered their guns. They looked as starving as the Schutzbund. Everyone was thin these days and nobody looked warm. For nearly two days they'd been out there; last night the temperature had been slightly raised, turning the snow to slush. Great clumps of it fell from the trees and disintegrated on the pavement. The whole of Karl-Marx-Hof appeared dirty and grey. Nothing moved but for the birds and the curtains which flapped outside the smashed out windows in the February breeze.

Anja and I were ushered into the college by members of the military with their guns half-cocked. Some of the windows were broken there, too, and the main hall was freezing since the boilers had all been disengaged. There were so many women, some wearing only their nightclothes and huddled in blankets, some nursing babies and comforting small children. I found a space and sat down on the floor with Anja. There was an unexpected atmosphere within the college walls, one of camaraderie and stoicism. Some of the women spontaneously broke into song, and there was an old lady with a withered arm who stood up on a chair in the centre of the hall and started reciting poetry, but her voice was quiet as a bird, drowned out by the sound of light artillery fire in the street. She wavered and cleared her throat; somebody chimed a spoon against a china mug. Outside the sound of shelling grew louder. She gave a little cough. The hall was shaking with heavy fire and some of the children started crying. A group of young ladies gathered around the old woman, one of them quivering so much she could hardly stand up. A few of the other women disappeared into the kitchen and made some thin broth out of whatever they could find. Later, they wheeled it into us in huge vats. We queued solemnly, letting the children go first. Nobody knew when the next meal would be.

On February 13th, the shelling stopped. In the distance, the dull thud of gunfire still continued but all of Karl-Marx-Hof was unnervingly quiet. The Schutzbund opened up their barricades and started to leave the municipal buildings with their hands in the air.

Anja threw off her blanket and shook her head. "Why are they giving up? Dollfuss will ban the Social Democrats because of this, and the trade unions. What will be left?"

"They can't ban a political party!" cried one of the women. "The election!"

"There won't be another election!" Anja laughed bitterly. As she turned to me I saw something in her eyes which made me shudder. "Something's coming," she whispered. It was almost a prophecy. "Something bigger than Dollfuss. Something bigger than the Democrats." She lay back down with an air of contentment that made me feel quite uneasy.

Who are you?

Chapter Fourteen

When at last they let us out onto the streets of Karl-Marx-Hof, the glare of the sun was blinding against the newly-fallen snow. Women pulled their shawls tightly around themselves, carrying their children and their few possessions. The sight we were greeted with was not the one any of us could have foreseen. Whole apartment blocks had been shot out and there were small fires still burning at the baths and the public library. The barbed wire and the fences hastily put up by the pickets were all gone. The strike was over, it seemed. Within a day, everyone would be trailing back to work with their tails between their legs. Broken glass lay glinting in the Viennese sunshine and dogs scavenged for food. How had this city of opera and Sachertorte slipped so swiftly into barbarism?

I couldn't even remember how it all began.

I broke free from Anja – I needed to calm myself, I told her, and I went for a walk along the Danube, far away from the allotments, down underneath the bridge which was covered in graffiti, where the bramble grew thick. And that was where I saw it: a line of makeshift tents along the banks and Roma sitting with lines cast into the water, fishing where there were breaks in the ice, with a bucket full of perch beside them.

"Selina!" It was Camlo. He called to me from his boat which was frozen into the water. "You're a sight for sore eyes!"

And though I was perished with cold, I felt a startling warmth inside me. I thought at first I might run across the ice to him, but of course it was far too thin and had already splintered and dissolved away in places. I ran up the steps, onto the bridge, over to the other side where he swept me up and scooped me onto his boat. There was a brace of ducks hanging in the doorway, which looked to have been shot recently. Inside, the boat had degenerated into much the same state as it was before Neomi and I had cleaned it. He brushed a load of newspapers and biscuit crumbs off his old armchair that I might sit down, but it was still greasy and covered in dog hairs. I stood where I was, glad of the warmth; the log burner raged hot at the other end of the boat.

"It's good to see you, Camlo," I said. "Where have you been?"

He only laughed. "When did you become my wife?" I felt my cheeks burning. "Just down the water a bit. I'm not one for laying roots... Did you miss me?"

"I came to see you," I said, looking at his unmade bed and the dirty socks and underpants which were strewn over the floor. "Just after Christmas, but you were gone."

"That's not what I asked, Selina."

He leaned in until his face came perilously close to mine. I felt his lips brush against my lips. I drew back.

"I don't like men!" I told him. "Not like that."

"I don't believe you."

Then I heard the bell jangling, at the front of the boat beside the rudder, and a little girl stepped into the cabin, closely followed by a woman who put a bag full of groceries down on the work surface and went and gave Camlo a kiss on the cheek. She wasn't an attractive woman, I considered. She was as plain and as ruddy-cheeked as any farm wife from Tyrol, and her child was dark with her forehead smeared with smut.

"I have to be going," I said. "I'm glad to see you're safe after all the trouble."

"Good day to you," said the woman.

I turned to walk away but when I looked back, Camlo was already curling his arm around her shoulder.

Chapter Fifteen

By May 1937, we were drawn into a state of fascism. They introduced the death penalty for rioting. Nobody who criticised the new regime remained in educational posts. There was no business which could have maintained its profits in these bleak times – not even Schwestern Flöge. It fell to me to break the news to the women. I went out onto the production room with my clipboard held stiffly in my hand. Fräulein Flöge remained ensconced in her office. Nobody looked up from their treadle. I sounded the horn and the noise from the machines wound itself down.

"I have bad news, I'm afraid, ladies," I heard myself say. I could feel my heart thudding in my chest; a woman at the back of the room dropped her thimble. "*Schwestern Flöge cannot sustain itself under the present circumstances,*" I read aloud from my clipboard. I struggled to stop my legs shaking, teetering as I was on my high heels. "*There will be a moderate remuneration package for anyone who wishes to volunteer – please speak to Fräulein Flöge directly – but I have to inform you that if there are not sufficient volunteers, difficult decisions will have to be made – on the basis of quality and quantity of work.*"

Nobody spoke, it was a sea of blank faces I was met with. I turned on my heels and marched back towards the office where Fräulein Flöge sat at her desk, just staring out of the window. I didn't venture outside the door for the rest of that day.

"Selina," she said to me when the lunchtime horn was sounded, "I shall also have to start seeing to my own administration once the dust has settled… I shall put you back on the machines as soon as the redundancies are sorted out. At least you will still have a wage." She put her hand on my shoulder.

When I left the factory that evening it was still warm, although the sun was quite low. Anja stood smoking beside the railings, talking to Rudi Martin.

"It's just as bad on the railway," he told her. "A quarter of the men will be gone by July, and the government say they're stopping unemployment benefits. There will be people dying in the gutter by winter, you wait…except the Jews who own all our newspapers and our banks. I imagine they'll keep their jobs!"

There was nothing to be done, he said. Even the unions had been disbanded.

I didn't know what to say. I felt awkward standing there with the pair of them, caught somehow in the gulf between the workers and the bourgeois, though why, I didn't know. I would be back sewing seams within a month.

Rudi had taken to wearing a uniform of late, a brown shirt. There were clusters of men all over Vienna dressed the same – thugs that was all, intimidating and assaulting Roma, Slavics and Jews.

"I don't know why you still even entertain him, Anja," I told her on our way back to Waldstrasse. "They're a bunch of bullies, that's all! And when you think how magnetic he used to be… What happened to him?"

She turned on me. "Life, Selina! Life happened! He's sick of it all and so am I."

Rudi started meeting Anja often at the factory gates and I would walk home alone. Some nights she didn't come back to our room at all. It was a testament to how indifferent I felt towards her. I was glad of the peace, glad to sleep on clean linen which didn't smell of her.

Chapter Sixteen

There was unemployment; there were food shortages; there was violence. Eight hundred people died. On the morning of 12 March, 1938, the 8th Army of the German *Wehrmacht* marched into Austria and were greeted by cheering German-Austrians with Nazi salutes, with Nazi flags which flew triumphantly on the breeze, and flowers, hundreds and hundreds of flowers – lilies and roses whose petals caught the sunlight and fell like confetti until the whole of the Strasse was carpeted in the most glorious colours of ivory and lavender and cherry. They called it the *Blumenkrieg* (war of flowers); it looked as if Klimt might have painted it himself.

The newspapers were awash with it; they talked of Hitler's car crossing the border in the afternoon at Braunau, his birthplace; the evening he arrived at Linz and was given an enthusiastic welcome in the City Hall.

It was three days later when he reached Vienna. I put down my newspaper and picked up my toast.

"Are you coming to see him today?" asked Anja. She was cleaner than I'd seen her for a long time, scrubbed like a new pin. She wore a starched shirt and shined shoes.

"What for?"

"I told you, Selina, something's coming." I'd never seen her eyes so bright.

It seemed the whole of the city had gathered on the Heldenplatz to listen to him speak. It was an unfortunate crowd he was met with that day with their thin clothes and wan expressions. We flooded in from Ringstrasse in our droves, waiting silently in the piazza in a sea of people which began within the arc of Neue Burg, with all its ostentation and grandeur, past the Festival Hall and the Leopold Wing of the Hofburg Palace and spilling out back onto the main street. The air was still that day and the sky watery and pale. Then there he was: Adolf Hitler, surrounded by a horde of officers. Among us there was not a sound, just for a second, then a cheer went up and the noise of it was deafening.

"The oldest eastern province of the German people shall be, from this point on, the newest bastion of the German Reich. As leader and chancellor of the German nation and Reich I announce to German history now the entry of my homeland into the German Reich. Certain foreign newspapers have said that we fell on Austria with brutal methods. I can only say: even in death they cannot stop lying. I have in the course of my political struggle won much love from my people, but when I crossed the former frontier into Austria there met me such a stream of love as I have never experienced. Not as tyrants have we come, but as liberators."

I sat in my room the next morning until ten drinking coffee and reading the newspapers. Eventually, I went downstairs, still in my housecoat with my hair tied in rags, to receive my post from the concierge. Some of the mailboxes were fuller than others, crammed with envelopes and postcards and packets, but on the top of each sat a crisp white envelope; two dozen white envelopes, which all looked exactly the same.

"Number fourteen." Jonas nodded politely as he handed me my letters. He looked as though he'd been crying. I put my hand out to him but he just shook his head and smiled a sad smile. I took his meaning and went back to my room, where I sat on the bed sifting through my mail. Sometimes I still thought there might be a letter from Leon or from Janika – silly really, I know. There was only a flyer from the Reich, a statement from my bank and a letter from my mother. I already knew its contents:

We are all fine; your father's joints seem a little better now that the worst of the winter is over; so-and-so's daughter is getting married; so-and-so has had a baby…

I sipped my coffee, I took up my letter opener and sliced open the white envelope. Inside was a ballot paper, a buff coloured rectangle of card. I read the words that were printed upon it:

Do you agree with the reunification of Austria with the German Reich that was enacted on 13 March 1938, and do you vote for the party of our leader Adolf Hitler?

Below it were two circles; a large one labelled *Yes* and a smaller one labelled *No*.

I was to cast my vote at the municipal college, the place where I'd learned to type not so many years ago. I thought of my teacher with her clipped accent and her manicured nails. The place was in a state of disrepair now; the railings were uprooted on either side of the steps and there were birds nesting in the eaves. Inside, the walls were still painted in the same tired sage green colour. I followed the arrows all the way round to the main hall. Officials were present directly beside the voting booths, Nazis wearing high boots and greatcoats. I placed my polling card on the shelf in the cubicle. There was nothing in there, only a pen attached to the wall with a piece of string. The guard stared in over my shoulder. I turned my head, our eyes met. I looked down at the buff square of card and the large circle with the word *YES* inside it. I took up the pen and put my cross next to it, handed it to the guard who nodded and put it in a pile with the rest. God forgive me.

When I went to call on Neomi later that day I found her frantically shoving a few clothes into a little suitcase. She was wearing her overcoat and was stuffing what bits of silver she had into the pockets.

"What are you doing?" I asked. I couldn't believe she

was leaving without even saying goodbye.

She snatched up an envelope from her sideboard. "My mother's cousin in Palestine has vouched for me. I have to go to the Emigration Office. I have to go today."

"Without even telling me?"

"There's no time, Selina. I have to go!"

I went with her to Prinz-Eugen-Strasse, to the Palais Albert Rothschild, lately seized by the Gestapo. Its gates were wide open and in the courtyard stood thousands of people, crammed in between the railings, up to their ankles in the sodden lawn. Through the first floor windows, crystal chandeliers could be seen still hanging in some of the suites and there was a marble staircase which swept away from the main entrance, but the people outside were saying the palace had been stripped of its riches, that the furniture and the art works were all gone.

The spring hadn't come early that year. I pulled my scarf tighter around my neck to keep out the cold. Neomi's eyes were drifting all over the throng of people. "We could be here for all week," she said. "They haven't allowed anyone inside for ages."

The clouds were hanging heavy that day. There were touts, men in brown shirts weaving their way through the crowd, pausing to speak with individuals, batting away the hands that reached out to them.

"They're paying them!" Neomi cried. Great drops of rain began falling from the sky, soaking her hair, making it stick to the sides of her face. "They're buying their way to the front of the line! Oh Selina!" Her eyes were wet with tears. "I haven't a Pfennig to my name!"

I hadn't any money either, just a few small coins left over from last week's wages. I left Neomi, with her overcoat drenched and her stockings all muddy and promised her I'd be back. There was my necklace of course. I took it from my drawer, still wrapped in its square of cloth and rushed it to the pawnbrokers on Bundesstrasse. But when I arrived there, Herr Levine was nowhere to be found. Instead his shop was crawling with Nazis who were scooping all of his stock into cloth sacks. None of them spoke to each other, they just went about their task mechanically. All of the warmth had gone from that place. The coffer where his jewellery had been housed was smashed and empty. Slivers of glass lay scattered on the shop floor. It was like a graveyard in there, although nobody was mourning, only picking over the carcasses like vultures. Outside, his windows had been daubed with obscenities and painted with a swastika. I clutched the necklace in my hand and backed away from the pawnbrokers in confusion. Anti-Semitism was not a new vogue in our civilised nation. It had always been there, bubbling just under the surface of our society, like a festering cesspit ready to erupt, and then somehow it did. It exploded in a way none of us could ever have dreamed of and it changed the world forever.

Perhaps I could scrape the fare together and pay Neomi's way to my family in Tyrol, or even Oberösterreich or Salzburg would have done. Anywhere that wasn't teaming with brownshirts or thieves.

I rushed back to my room, virtually snatching the key from Jonas Lehner. I emptied out the contents of my chest of drawers out onto the floor, rifled through my jacket pockets and groped around inside the upholstery of my sofa. All I came up with was four pfennigs.

When I arrived back at Prinz-Eugen-Strasse, the gathering had swelled and spilled out onto the street. There was a queue of people which trailed right the way around the grounds. I couldn't see Neomi anywhere; it would have been impossible to find her in this crowd. She would make her way back to Waldstrasse in the end, I considered. She'd have to wait until the end of next week. If I could avoid Herr Auer and maybe just live on potatoes for a few days. That was it; that was what I should do.

I managed to keep to my plan just as long as Thursday, by which time there was still no sign of Neomi. We'd only just returned from our lunch breaks and resumed our work when Fräulein Flöge burst into the production room and thrust open the shutters at the sash windows.

"Oh no!" she cried. "Oh dear God!"

The machines stopped clacking and a crowd gathered quickly around Fräulein Flöge.

"What is it?" asked one of the girls.

"It is Frau Liep," she said. Across the street at the smart town-houses an old lady and a bent-up old gentleman were being led out of their house by the Gestapo. The lady could hardly move, whether from the swollenness of her ankles or by sheer fear I couldn't tell, but her feet wouldn't go anywhere and she stood there rooted to the spot. Then one of the men slapped her harshly and they pulled her along with her legs dangling limply. We all fell silent and stood there to the last woman with ashen faces.

Officers swarmed into the property and came out with sacks bulging with their belongings, which they hurled onto the waggon. They started coming out with flat rectangular objects covered in sheets: the paintings from the Lieps' collection. Our painting, *The Women Friends*... They had it. They had Janika.

I backed away from the window with my hand over my mouth, not knowing whether she'd escaped over the border, whether she was dead or alive even. "The painting!" I cried. The pain of it was so sharp it was as if someone had stuck a knife in my chest.

Fräulein Flöge turned on me with tears swimming in her eyes and her face as pale as a corpse. "They are human beings! I don't give a damn about the paintings. Now get back to work, all of you!"

The crowd dispersed and we all went slowly back to our tables. The machines began to rattle again but we worked on without speaking. I carried on working in that way, in silence, with my belly rumbling with hunger, until at last the bell sounded to mark the end of the day. I folded up my unfinished garment and put it back in the basket ready for the morning. I walked all the way back to Waldstrasse, past the coffee houses and patisseries. None of them held any pull for me; all I could think of was the train fare. I'd heard people were crammed into the trains like sardines, standing all the way almost suffocating each other, just to get to the countryside, though none of them had any family or hope of work there. Jews weren't even allowed to occupy jobs since the beginning of the new regime, not ones wanted by the rest of the population at any rate. My head was full of these thoughts until, as I turned onto Waldstrasse, there looked to be a scuffle outside our block of rooms. I could hear screaming and a little boy clinging to his mother's apron crying, "I don't want to see it."

A man was on the floor, surrounded by brownshirts who were stamping all over his body while he choked and emptied his bowels. I heard the woman yelling, "Stop! There's a four-year-old here." Telling them off, as if they were children. And it worked for a second, too; they seemed so shocked that they stood still for a moment, panting from the exertion of it all. I rushed nearer to the man on the floor as he heaved himself onto all fours and I stopped dead in my tracks. It was Jonas Lehner. One of them swung back his boot and kicked him squarely in the face. He fell flat on his back, stretched out. I thought they surely must have killed him. People scattered and the brownshirts all ran away laughing. Then there was just me and Jonas all alone on Waldstrasse in the sickening quiet.

I don't know how he ever managed to get to his feet, but he did, and he wandered aimlessly like one of those shell-shocked young men sent home gibbering from the front in 1918.

"Jonas," I said, and I put my hand on his back so as to steady him. He flinched under my touch. "It's me, Selina, do you know me?"

He nodded but he looked right through me. I held my handkerchief up to him. There was blood seeping from his mouth.

"My glasses," he kept saying. I don't know whether he knew he'd soiled himself.

"I can see them," I said, noticing a pair of spectacles lying some metres away in the middle of the pavement. I'm going to take you to them now, alright, Jonas? I won't let you go."

"Are they broken?" he was asking. He sounded like a little boy. I didn't think they were. "Why did they do that to you, Jonas?" I asked. "You're not even Jewish."

"I'm a homosexual," he reminded me as I helped him up the stairs. As he turned to look at me, his expression was most grave.

"Selina, you must tell your lady friend not to come here anymore. They'll say you're a prostitute or a communist, put you to work in a brothel in one of their camps. They'll round you up. I've heard rumours about what they do to the women. Terrible things. You mustn't give them cause for suspicion."

I nodded, feeling his words weighing heavily on me. "My parents have a farm in Tyrol," I told him. "I'm just saving up until I have the fare. You could come with me, and Neomi…"

He looked at me with tears in his eyes.

"Neomi's gone," he said. "She came back here this morning and they took her right away. Seventy thousand arrested so far, they say, from the countryside as well as the city. There's no point going anywhere."

I felt a chill run up the back of my neck. When I went back to my room I found it had been ransacked. My necklace was gone.

I spent the remainder of my wages on absinthe that night. It was the only way I could get any sleep. But as soon as I closed my eyes, I was back in the painting again. Janika was naked and there were men in brownshirts grabbing at her breasts and shoving their guns between her legs while she cried and begged them to stop. And I ran from that place in my silk robe and turban through the streets of Vienna with Klimt's birds squawking around my head. But as fast as I ran, the soldiers marched after me and at every turn there were more, until I was completely surrounded by men. One of them pulled off my robe and I was naked. I heard Janika crying. I woke up with a start, still holding the empty bottle of absinthe and reached for my packet of cigarettes from my purse.

What had become of my life? Cigarettes, absinthe, wine, falling asleep on my own or with a woman who I detested, stitching silk dresses – dresses that the likes of me would never be able to afford in a million years. That was all there was to show for my forty years. If only I'd known how short life was and how precious, when I boarded that steam locomotion from Tyrol! I'd wasted it all, and there was no way I could get it back. Then the fear came, enveloping me in its cloak, swallowing me up. They had the painting. *They* had it, and God knows what they might do to me should it ever betray me.

But my thoughts were soon shaken from me. There was some kind of commotion going on in the street. I smelled burning oil. It was only faint. I pulled back the blind and saw that the night sky was as rosy as a sunset. The flames licked the heavens like the devil's tongue…

The Danube. I put my coat on and ran down Waldstrasse in my bare feet, hearing the cracking of fire and the screams and shouts from beyond the allotments. Over the little vegetable patches I ran with the bramble tearing at my feet and the sodden earth oozing between my toes. The whole place was bathed in orange light. As I neared the fence at the canal side, I could hear women shrieking and men shouting. The boats of the Roma were on fire. Everything had gone up like brushwood: the oil drums and the washing hanging on the rope, the fishing tents on the bank. Everything was alight. Shards of ash flew out from the inferno and trembled on the breeze like snowflakes. I heard Camlo shouting Lenza's name over the roaring fire and the sirens. He ran into the plumes of smoke that were pouring from his boat, with his torso shining and smeared with soot, but was beaten back by the scorching heat. Then everything was still but for the fire.

I held my breath, feeling tears stinging my eyes.

"Camlo!" I yelled. Nothing. I looked about me for help. Thick clouds billowed out across the water. Just at the moment it seemed all was lost, finally, he stumbled coughing and retching from the blaze and collapsed on the banks of the Danube. I saw a figure running away, up the tow path underneath the bridge; a tall man, sturdily built. From the thicket a woman leapt out and joined him, quickening her stride to keep pace with him.

"Camlo!" I said again as I went to his side and knelt beside him on the ground. I looked again along the tow path, which trailed away into the dark. The two forms were unmistakable: Rudi and Anja. Behind them were yet more, a horde of shadowy figures leaping from the undergrowth, whooping and laughing as they disappeared into the night.

Chapter Seventeen

I don't know how I managed to get him back through the allotments and along Waldstrasse, let alone up to my room. It was all he could do to support his own weight. Once inside, he flopped down upon my bed with the back of his hand across his face and his eyes shut. It was only when I lit the lamp that I saw his burns: one in a huge crescent shape across his chest where his St. Christopher must have overheated and swung about his neck and another around his wrist underneath his bracelet. I fetched my box of bandages and lint from the kitchen cupboard. At least I could see to his wounds. He didn't flinch as I dabbed them with antiseptic or as I took the chain from around his throat. I taped a dressing to his chest and wound a bandage around his wrist and over his hand. It was the strong hand of a working man. I turned out the light and lay down with him upon the bed. We stayed like that, sleeplessly and without words, until dawn came creeping in through the blinds and the odd engine in the street below mingled with birdsong outside my window.

I made him some tea and gave him a crust of bread with a little lemon curd, which I passed to him as he propped himself up on his elbow. He took just a morsel of the bread and sat staring at it with dead eyes.

"We were like brothers," he said. "What did he ever do to anyone?"

I shook my head. "These are senseless times. I think there will be another war."

"You've cut your foot, you know," he told me.

He held out his hand and I sat back down on the bed so that he might take a look at it.

He held my ankle in his hand and turned it slowly. "You've just torn it on some bramble or something. Look at you, Miss Barefoot Slippers! I thought it was only the likes of us who went around with no shoes!" He pressed the sole of my foot against his lips, though it was filthy and caked in mud.

When I looked back at him, he was crying, silently, with tears trickling down his cheeks. "I'm scared, Selina." He stood up and smoothed back his hair, which had escaped from its band and hung wildly about his face. "I want to go back to the canal, see what's left."

"You're in shock," I said. "I don't think that's a good idea."

"I've got to go."

He didn't even have anything to wear. I went downstairs to Jonas's apartment and asked if I might have one of his shirts. He limped around his living room, sifting through the mounds of clothes which were heaped up on the arm chairs and writing desk.

"Are you alright?" I asked.

He nodded, pulling a plain linen shirt from the bottom of one of the piles. "I never imagined life would come to this."

I pressed his hand. "These are dark times. They can't last forever."

I changed into some dungarees and went with Camlo. The streets were deathly quiet that day; the news-stands were all locked up and the grills on most of the shops hadn't been taken down. The delivery boys and the stream of men going to work on the railway were conspicuous by their absence. When we arrived at the canal side, the air was still thick with the stench of fire. All that remained were two empty hulks, charred remains where the boats used to be. The others had either been salvaged or floated away down the Danube. They were nowhere to be seen. Blackened oil drums littered the banks, whose grasses were scorched and scarred with fire. That place, which the Roma had filled with the music of the harmonica and the violin, with laughter and the scent of goose fat and wood smoke, all turned to ashes.

I held his hand. I saw his eyes searching over the wreckage. "I should go onto Lenza's boat," said Camlo. "I can't face it, Selina. I don't know what I'd find."

"Don't do it," I said.

We strolled back to Waldstrasse still holding hands. We must have looked like lovers, I supposed. "What about the woman who was on your boat that time?" I asked. "And the girl?"

Camlo snorted. "Aishe? She comes and goes. She's long gone this time. I've not seen her for ages. The girl's not mine."

"I thought she might have been your wife." I said.

He snorted again. "You know when you've just known someone a long time and it's easy? It was easier to keep going with her even though I wasn't happy. Easier than taking the risk of finding someone new."

I took the cigarettes from my pocket, lit them both, and held one out for him to take.

"I don't know where I'll go," he said.

"You could come with me."

His eyes were full of melancholy as he turned to me. "I don't know – they're herding people in like cattle."

I shrugged and dug my hands into my pockets. "You'll have to. There's no way out of Vienna." I took his hand again and led him away from the water. There was nothing left for him.

We went back to my room. I poured us some absinthe, and we sat side by side on the sofa.

"You drink too much, Selina," he told me.

I liked it. What else was there? And yet, perhaps he was right.

"I've got something to ask you," he began, swirling his absinthe around in his glass. "It would only be an arrangement; it wouldn't have to be forever."

I put my hand on his; I knew what he was going to ask, I

thought. "It could help us both out, perhaps," I said. "You are talking about us getting married, aren't you?" I wasn't sure about it. Camlo was a good man and he obviously cared for me, that was what made it worse; I'd spent half my life loving a woman, what if one day another one came along? If I hurt him I'd never forgive myself.

"I'm sorry," he said. Tears were already welling again in his eyes. "If I were to take an Austrian wife they might... I —"

"Shhhhh." I put my finger to his lips. "It's alright. I'll do it."

"Really?" The relief in his voice was almost tangible.

I nodded. "But there are lots of people doing the same. It's all a mad rush before they pass the new law. There will be questions, there's a process; we'll have to convince them we're a real couple. Promise me you're not already married to that woman."

"To Aishe? I told you, she's not my wife. She's just someone I have a nice time with now and again. But mostly we have a horrible time. We fight like cat and dog. She's drunk more than she is sober and she's got a mouth like a sewer... She's not like you." He almost laughed. "You're a tough nut to crack, Selina Brunner."

I got to my feet and was unfastening the straps of my dungarees. I let them fall to the floor and unbuttoned my blouse.

"What are you doing?" he asked.

"You need to know what I look like," I said. "If they ask you, you'll need to know. Take your clothes off."

Camlo stood up and slid the braces from his shoulders so they hung loosely around his hips. He undid the top three buttons, put his hand to the back of his neck and pulled Jonas's shirt off over his head, unbuttoned his fly and let his trousers fall to the floor.

He was wiry underneath his clothes with sinewy thighs and a line of soft dark hair trailing all the way from the middle of his chest down to his belly button, which was quite deep-set in his tight stomach.

"You need to take it all off," I said, "so I can see it all."

I took off my brassiere and knickers, feeling my breath quicken. It was like sitting for Klimt all those years ago as he contemplated me, not in any leering way at all, just studying me, with his brown eyes wandering all over my body.

"You're very beautiful," he said.

I thought somehow I should cover myself.

He shrugged and took off the rest of his own clothes, and there we were, two virtual strangers, standing naked, staring at each other in a room in the slum that was Karl-Marx-Hof.

"Can we stay like this a while?" he asked, and he picked up the half-finished bottle of absinthe and took it to my bed.

We lay like that silently, passing the bottle between us. But as I put the bottle to my lips, the taste of it was quite unpleasant. I'd put aside my knives and my constant scrubbing only to replace it with wine and this sickly green devil. I put the bottle down on the floor and listened to the sound of Camlo's heart beating as I lay my head on his chest.

"Was there never a man?" he asked.

"Once. His name was Leon. It was a long time ago, back in Tyrol." I found myself shocked, saying his name without feeling the sting of it.

"What happened?" He put his finger underneath my chin and lifted my face towards his.

"He married someone else."

He kissed me. It had been such a long time since I'd been kissed by a man, to be held in arms that were strong and unyielding, to feel the urgency of a man, to feel quite helpless. He ran his fingers gently down the curve of my back, let his lips wander down my neck and over my breasts.

Before I even had chance to stop myself I was pulling him closer to me and he was moving inside me. I wrapped my fingers around the back of his neck and my legs around his waist. I never wanted him to stop.

Chapter Eighteen

We walked the next day through Rathauspark with its neat lawn and beds bursting with irises and yellow tulips. The fountain sparkled in the morning sun though the sky was still pale as topaz. I'd always thought Vienna such an ugly place, but it was only now, as I felt it falling all around me that I realised how beautiful it really was. I gazed at the Johann Strauss monument, whose bronze was corroded in places and coated in a blue-green layer. What had happened to our city of bright lights, of waltzes and coffee piped with cream?

As we trod the path, hand in hand, to City Hall, I became conscious of the glare of strangers upon me, the Austrian woman with the Roma in the borrowed shirt. A group of young men came walking towards us, chatting and laughing then falling quiet as they drew near. They didn't step aside for us and in the end we had to walk around them on the grass; it was only a small thing, I supposed. As we approached a woman reading on a bench, she looked up from her book, seeming unable to take her eyes off us. Even after we'd passed, when I looked over my shoulder her gaze did not falter. Worst were the children, a group of them engaged with a hoop and stick.

"Stinking gypsies!" one of the little girls cried after us, and a boy spat a ball of phlegm onto the ground. Yet through it all, Camlo kept walking with his held high, though his grasp upon my hand grew ever tighter.

The City Hall loomed above us with all the majesty of the great Gothic cathedrals, with its towers piercing the pallid sky. Its clock had not yet struck nine, but already trailed around the side of the building was a long line of people. Most were Austrian women like me, with men of questionable heritage, although for a few couples the pairing was the opposite way around. We waited with for the bell to toll. Sometimes a soft mutter could be heard over the noise of the fountains, but mostly not.

At length, we were led into a great vestibule with a polished floor which was mostly covered by a Turkish rug in shades of burnt orange and ochre. There were two pointed arched windows at the far side of the hall which rose up from ceiling to floor and a chandelier hanging from the ceiling. The women were separated from the men, each of us led into small rooms off the main hall. I was taken into a chamber without windows which was painted white and furnished simply with a wooden table and chairs and a screened off area to the right. A man in a suit sat at the table, beside a nurse in uniform. I stood there clutching my handbag, just looking at them, not knowing quite what I should do.

"Sit, sit," said the man eventually, looking up from the pile of papers on his desk. I pulled out the chair he was gesticulating towards and seated myself at the table opposite him. The nurse smiled at me, but it was an uneasy smile. "I take it you have come for a marriage licence? Name?"

I felt the tension tighten in my shoulders. "Selina Brunner."

His face seemed to soften. "Please try and relax, Fräulein Brunner. These are difficult times; there are new regulations in place as I am sure you can appreciate... And your fiancé – his name?"

"Camlo Ziga."

He looked at me steadily over the top of his spectacles and laid down his pen. There was a pointed silence, as if he was considering something. "Hungarian?" he suggested at last. He cast a glance at the nurse who nodded for me to go on.

"Yes," I replied cautiously. "He was born in Hungary."

"But he has lived in Vienna all his life?"

"Yes."

He picked up his pen again and started scribbling on his form. "And you met where?"

"A friend introduced us. He used to help her on her allotment."

"A gardener, then? By means of occupation?"

I nodded.

"And would you say he was clean?"

I nodded again.

"Home-loving or inconstant?"

"Oh, he is reliable," I assured him.

"Fond of children?"

I looked to the nurse for some help. She bit down hard on her bottom lip and turned her face away.

"We've spoken about it, but I'm forty. Perhaps it's no longer possible."

He considered for a moment. "It is not unheard of. We have a medical officer to assist in determining those matters."

I looked towards the modesty screen which sectioned off the room. Klimt's studio sprang sharply and vividly to my mind with its half-naked women and the lady with her hair in a bun who undressed me, with Janika who had lounged in front of all and lost herself in the act of self-love. I thought of these things; they were all so very long ago, a different life.

"But everything seems to be in order," he said at last.

"Thank you." The tears clouded my eyes.

"They are calling unions like yours a *Resistance of the Heart*, I believe, Fräulein. You are a very brave woman indeed."

"I'm not brave!" I protested. "I'm an ordinary woman – a seamstress from Tyrol."

He only smiled. "One day, my dear, you will realise the enormity of what you have done here." He stood up and gestured towards the door. "I hope everything goes well for you, Fräulein Brunner."

I waited outside the shadow of the City Hall until the sun

125

climbed right up to its summit and all shade died away. I waited so long I wondered if I'd ever see Camlo again. The park was not as it used to be. Workers from the municipal buildings used to take their lunch in the grounds; the paths were usually dotted with cyclists at their leisure. Now everywhere seemed empty, but for the people with a particular purpose and the few children who should have been at school. Finally, I saw his silhouette emerging from the building, the sinewy outline I'd come to recognise.

"How did it go?" I asked. I went to touch his hand but something made me check myself.

He gave a little shrug. "Alright, I think. But it cost me my gold bracelet." His smile was boyish and wry as he pushed up his shirt sleeve to reveal a bare arm. "We'll soon see, Selina. It's out of our hands."

On the way home, we stopped in at the café – the one I'd been to with Neomi with its plastic tablecloths and Formica counter where the pastries were kept under a glass cover. The bell rang at the door as Camlo opened it for me. The place was almost empty; only a couple of old ladies sat it the corner, sharing a pot of coffee and an apple strudel. Camlo pulled out my chair for me and took my coat. I'd quite forgotten all those small touches, the ways a man has of making a woman feel special.

We took a seat next to the window, which looked grubby behind the net curtains.

"How long do you think they'll take?" he asked. "To decide about the licence?"

"God knows. We must carry on as a normal engaged couple. As you said, it's out of our hands."

"It won't be so bad, will it?" He reached over the table and stroked my hand.

"What's that?"

"Carrying on as an engaged couple."

At a loss for what to say, I looked at the menu. *Perhaps some rabbit stew.* But the owner didn't move from her position behind that Formica counter. She stood solidly with her arms folded and a stony look on her face. One of the old ladies dropped a sugar cube into her coffee. I heard the discordant chink of the spoon against the china as she stirred her drink. At last I cleared my throat. "Could we order some food, please?"

Still the lady stood statuesquely. Finally, she turned her head and stared at something seemingly off in the distance. I followed her gaze to a sign on the door: *NO JEWS, NO GYPSIES.*

I snatched up my coat. "Your windows need cleaning."

"Apologies," said Camlo to the lady. He reached in his pocket and laid two Pfennigs gently down onto the table.

I stormed out onto the street and stared at him in disbelief as he dipped out of the café, feeling tears welling in my eyes. I took a cigarette from my purse.

He brushed my cheek with the back of his hand. "It's better to deal with these people gracefully, Selina... And you don't need to smoke either. It doesn't suit you." He put his arm around my shoulder. "Don't waste your tears on her. If she wants to live her life full of hatred, leave her to it!" He stood himself up straight. "My stew's better than hers anyway."

By the time we got back, Karl-Marx-Hof was surrounded by so many SS men with their austere black jackets and boots, who amassed at every street corner and blocked off all the exits. There was the crack of gunshots in some of the tenements, but more so in the hospital where nurses came streaming out in tears. People were being ordered from their dwellings. Some of them, wearing only the clothes on their back, were being dragged out by the SS. Together they were marched through the tangle of streets, the washing still strung between the apartment blocks. A man wearing working attire ran out from the crowd and was gunned down in the middle of the road, his back bursting open and streaming with blood as he stopped in his tracks and fell to the ground. There were screams from the throng of people, some of whom tried to rush to his side but were dragged back and beaten.

A cry rang out from the windows. "Good riddance,

Jews!"

In procession they were taken away. There was nothing we could do except stand there dumbly while we turned our heads away. I'd seen so much, nothing even seemed shocking any more. Nothing seemed real. It was as if I'd turned to stone.

It wasn't until I arrived home that the shock of it hit me. I stood shaking, freezing cold. Camlo fetched the blanket from my bed and wrapped me in it, chaffing my shoulders. But it did nothing to block out the memory of the gunfire or the screaming, or of the man falling dead on the ground. He made me a cup of sweet tea and lit a cigarette for me.

I didn't want anything to eat but it was dusk already and I hadn't touched a morsel all day.

Camlo said I'd need to keep my strength up if I was to survive. He hung his trousers over the back of the chair to dry. He busied himself in the kitchen, wearing just his long johns and shirt, chopping up celeriac for the stock. Soon, I smelled the sour aroma of onion. He'd been quiet since leaving the café but he looked dignified still as he worked with his crooked knife and took down the rabbit from its hook. I put my feet up on the little sofa.

I couldn't say how long I'd been lost with my thoughts when I was roused by a knock at the door. When I opened it, there was Jonas, a sorry sight stood there, still with blood caked in his hair and crusted on his lip. His eyes were swollen and black. It was only by his dress and demeanour that I recognised him at all.

"Selina, I wondered if I could have a word with you."

In the kitchen, Camlo started humming a tune, one which I recognised from the days on the allotment when he and Lenza helped Neomi with the coop. Perhaps he did it to allow the older man a sense of privacy, or simply to make him aware I wasn't alone. I couldn't tell. He pushed back his hair and seasoned the pot with salt and pepper.

Jonas lowered his head. "I was thinking, Selina that perhaps…just until Vienna comes to its senses, that, well…

that you might agree to marry me. It would be in name only, I wouldn't expect that—"

"I'm already promised to someone else." I looked over my shoulder to Camlo whose eyes met mine. He almost looked sad. "I'm sorry, Jonas."

He nodded, too quickly and for too protracted a length of time. "It was just an idea. I'm sorry. I can see you're busy; I'll show myself out."

The door closed quietly behind him.

"It isn't your fault, Selina." Camlo came out of the kitchen, wiping his hands on a tea towel. "The world's gone mad; it's not down to you."

I buried my face in his chest. "Why does it feel so bad?"

He held me close. "That rabbit won't be ready for a long while yet."

Then he kissed me and I forgot about all the unpleasantness of the day. Everything just seemed to disappear, but for me and him. I needed him; I clung to him as he undressed me, as he kissed me down the curve of my neck, made love to me on the floor. All I could feel was the rhythm of him and the warmth of his body against mine. We held each other tight – two frightened, desperate people, grasping around for those few precious moments in the dark.

Every day I went downstairs to check the mail but there was nothing for me. Jonas wasn't there in the little bureau and the letters were sitting in a great heap on the counter, growing steadily by the day. It was the following Monday that I sifted through the mail, and there it was – the telegram from the registrar.

Shakily, I held it in my hands. They'd approved the marriage licence.

Chapter Nineteen

There was a queue of people on the platform: lots of couples. The women mostly wore scarves and long coats. Some of them were carrying small luggage bags while the men had larger suitcases and trunks. The SS were guarding the waiting train. The officers were seated at a row of tables, checking the papers of those boarding. A woman wearing a fur coat was roughly plucked from the queue and pushed in the direction of another crowd of people who were being detained by soldiers. At the front of the line there was a man with his head bent forwards in some kind of muffled conversation with the officer. He tried to pass something to him but the officer thrust it back into his hand. They beat him right there on the platform.

The queue ebbed slowly away, people being either allowed to board or held back. We reached the front. The officer at the desk stared at me with steely eyes, harsh against his pallid skin and slicked back hair. I shifted from side to side.

"Papers," he said finally.

Camlo took the marriage licence from his breast pocket together with the other identification papers.

I licked my lips, feeling the dryness upon them and in my mouth.

The officer looked down at the licence and then back up at me. He called to one of the other SS men who came to inspect the documents. He walked slowly up to the table, eyed both of us and then took the licence from his comrade. I saw his eyes flitting back and forwards over the page. He held his hand out for the rest of the papers. I felt the sweat trickle down the back of my neck. He folded the documents up neatly.

"Have a pleasant journey, Fräulein." He handed the documents back to Camlo. "Herr Ziga." His mouth twisted into an unfathomable little smile as he flicked his head towards the waiting train.

I left Vienna in 1938, travelling towards that distant place which was Tyrol, on a steam locomotion which wound its way through the Austrian countryside, with its lush hills and its pastel villages. I sat in the airless carriage with the windows up and the grey veil of smoke swirling past me as the train gathered speed, racing away from Vienna. To my left was a narrow corridor where people hurried back and forth in search of seats.

"Entschuldigen Sie bitte," they mumbled as they navigated past one another. There was a rectangular mirror opposite and a rolled up blind at the window, racks for luggage, a glass lamp whose shade had yellowed with heat.

I could hear a muffled conversation somewhere. "God knows where they have taken them or what they might do."

I was sick of it. I rested my head against the juddering window frame and watched as the forests grew darker. The train rushed under a tunnel which had been carved out of the mountain side. Everything went black.

"They call unions like this a *Resistance of the Heart,*" I whispered to Camlo.

I felt his mouth close to my ear and the warmth of his breath against my skin. "*Of the heart*? Then I could be forgiven for thinking you might love me? Perhaps you're not such a tough nut to crack after all, Miss Barefoot Slippers!"

The train emerged screaming from the tunnel and my reflection became vivid in the glass. And also vivid was Camlo's reflection, his dark ringlets and his chocolatey eyes. I was no longer that young girl, who'd left home with only her dreams. No longer the model, trapped in a painting, with a phoenix, a raven and a red-eyed swan, clinging to a woman who cared nothing for me…

I was free.

I turned from the window and took him in my arms. Sometimes love can creep up on a person, even on a woman like me who thought her heart was completely shut. Sometimes it can be stronger than hatred and malice and fear.

Sometimes all you have to do is let it in.

THE END

References

http://en.wikipedia.org/wiki/Emilie_Floge
http://en.wikipedia.org/wiki/Gustav_Klimt
Partsch, S, 2006, *Gustav Klimt, Painter of Women,* London, Prestel Publishing
Whitford, F, 1990, *Klimt*, London, Thames and Hudson Ltd.
firstworldwar.com/features/minorpowers_at.htm
www.thefullwiki.org/Austrofascism
www.thefullwiki.org/Austrian_Civil_War

Fantastic Books
Great Authors

CROOKED
CAT

Meet our authors and discover
our exciting range:

- Gripping Thrillers
- Cosy Mysteries
- Romantic Chick-Lit
- Fascinating Historicals
- Exciting Fantasy
- Young Adult and Children's
  Adventures

18871075R00083

Printed in Great Britain
by Amazon